You Never Leave Him

Wendy Oliver

Published by New Generation Publishing in 2025

ISBN: 978-1-83563-879-8

www.newgeneration-publishing.com

New Generation Publishing

Acknowledgements

Thank you to Astrid Reid and Sam Kaye for typing and editing the manuscript, and assisting with design. Thanks to Rachel Silkin for help with distribution.

Part One

It is how many years, I wonder, since I left Stoke Newington? It feels like twenty, like more than twenty. Fifteen in fact. I have never been back, but sometimes I hear it mentioned on the radio, at election time for instance; and recently, on a train-seat, I found an abandoned 'West Indian World'. The news was much the same as it had always been: police harassment, beauty contests, new business ventures asking for support. One of the wedding couples showed a black man and a white girl, a handsome couple, a showpiece for a multicultural society, you might say.

It could have been Clyde and Sylvie, that wedding couple. Except that Clyde did not marry Sylvie. I am sure, looking back, that the idea never crossed his mind. But Sylvie used to wear white a lot when she was with Clyde, to emphasise the colour in her skin, make it look more golden, nearer to his own colour. After he left her she wore dark hues, brown and grey, and when she and I went our separate ways she gave me those sombre clothes. (I needed them, but that is another story.) But for a few months Sylvie was bridal.

I was wearing Sylvie's brown chiffon dress and grey velvet jacket the first time I went to the Worldwide Evangelical Mission Chapel in Kingsland High Street. It was there, many weeks later, when I was trusted, that I heard sung the praises of May, Clyde's mother who had Gone to Glory. Marvin's mother too, of course. May had supported Clyde and his younger brother throughout their childhood by garment-machining. Clyde himself had once told me of his early memories of the heavy industrial machine that shook their basement flat. In the quiet intervals when his mother rearranged the cloth he would hear her voice, softly, for she had been singing under the din of the machine.

"Mammy singin' hymns, darlin'", she would say.

By the time I got to know him, Clyde was a graduate and teacher, in other words, a prodigy. For a young Black Briton, as the politicians put it, from a working class, one-parent family, as the sociologists put it, to graduate in English Literature from Queen Mary's College, London University, in 1970, was prodigious. But there it is: not every man can be Everyman. He was, in his own neighbourhood, a sort of paragon. But the ladies at the Evangelical Mission were not at ease with him. It hurt them that this good and clever man, who had been a good and clever child, had stopped coming to Chapel with his mother as soon as he was old enough to choose. One Sunday morning, as I stood on the steps outside the Chapel, talking to one of the ladies, Clyde's car drove past and he waved to both of us. We both waved back, exclaiming and smiling, then my companion dropped her hand and frowned.

"Clyde a fine man, yes Lord," she said. "May would be proud of him. But you know, it not right for one child so favoured and the other so bad."

"Have they got different fathers?" I asked. In straw hats, pastel dresses and pearl-grey suits the churchgoers milled around us, talking and embracing. My questions seemed to shock Doris.

"Oh no, May not like that! That woman true Gospel Christian, she not yield the temptation of the flesh!"

"I'm sorry. I only wondered if she had been married twice."

Now Doris seemed annoyed. "May not married," she said stiffly. "She was true Gospel Christian, but that man no good, him sneer at the Gospel of Christ. Him not marry her, even when she make him two baby." Her voice warmed again. "You know how she get money to bring children over here? Not from him! Oh no! She go down fish dock every morning, gut fish for saltfish, take it for saltin' in basket on her head." She laughed a little, forgetting me. "Well, why not, Lord? Me done same thing, long ago."

"How old were the boys when they came here?"

"Let me see now, Marvin two, Clyde six. We meet here, in this Chapel, first Sunday she come to England. Both boys with she. Clyde quiet and good, true Christian child —" she twisted her lips, for had we not

3

both just seen the true Christian child drive past the Chapel - "But Marvin!" She recollected herself, threw up her hands. "That terrible baby, Miss, me tell you! Him scream, fight Mama, pull out her hairs in him fist, make she cry. We have to stop service till she take him out. Hannah say: it strange place, he only little baby, we not say anything wrong of him or him Mama. Hannah have Selwyn with her, 'bout one, two year old, me have Winston and Claudette both little as well. I talkin' 'bout when we was all young." Her voice trailed away. Selwyn and Winston and Claudette no longer came to Chapel either.

Another Sunday Hannah, an older woman, talked to me on the way from church. Our ways took us both down Camleigh Road. Hannah told me I had a fine voice: a compliment which pleased me more than any other could have done. I had never thought about my voice: it had no part in my efforts and successes and failures. So it was like being given money I hadn't worked for. Hannah remembered that May had had a fine voice too, and had known every hymn by heart.

"But oh, Miss, it make you heart break to see she try sing Marvin to sleep! She rock him in she arms, she talk him like a baby; no good." She pointed her forefinger and altered the pitch of her voice. "I'm talkin' 'bout when him big boy, six, seven year old, already start school! Already in trouble at school, right from first day. Always fightin', always hurtin' other children. But holler like a baby if they hit him back.

Poor May, she always goin' up the school, see headmaster, and she can't afford time off the machine, you see. It all money wasted. Oh Miss, she have a cross to bear with that child! An' not just see headmaster! No, she have to take him Child Guidance Clinic, once a week, six months. That two buses you know, Green Lanes, near the waterworks, then sit an' wait maybe half an hour, even before she see man."

But hearing this, that day, I failed to be impressed. I had no child myself, not even an easy one; I had never had to support anyone else, sometimes not even myself. That bus routes and half hours in waiting rooms might cause misery; might, over the years, wear the soul away, was unknown to me. Instead of being impressed, I asked if the child psychiatrist had done any good.

Hannah sighed. "No, Miss, him no help, no more than anybody else. Him ask May if she beat Marvin. She tell him, yes, one time, because Doris tell her it do him good. She beat him one time and locked him in coal cellar. I remember it because I was visiting with her. Oh Miss, how him holler! Him near break the door down, and only five year old! White lady next door come ask what the matter, says she go ring police. May tell her, no. Then she let Marvin out. Well, anyway, May tell all this to that man at Clinic. An' do you know, Miss, ever after that, every time she go, that man tell her: you must stop beatin' Marvin. May say: I am stop, I just beat him that one time. But that man not hear her, him could be deaf. Him jus' keep on sayin': you must stop beating Marvin. Every time she go. An' next breath him say: Marvin needs proper discipline. May ask him: what proper discipline she ought to do, an' that man say: that is for you to discover. Imagine it, miss! I not believe my ears when May first tell me. She weep when she tell me. She sit in me kitchen, leave that machine for once, and jus' weep. "

I could feel this alright; I too had suffered under double binds: do it and don't do it! But even so I couldn't take my part properly in talking to Hannah. She was treating me as her confidant, her equal, on the grounds that I sang hymns well and went to her Chapel. She was seeing more in me than was really there. I felt as if I were fraudulent through no fault of my own.

As we turned the corner by the Greek off-licence I said, "Couldn't Clyde have helped her? Seen to Marvin at school, and - and - put him to bed sometimes? Things like that?"

She looked at me as if I had made some unrepeatable, absurd suggestion. As if I had asked why May hadn't hired a nanny.

"Clyde no good to him," she said briefly. "Too different. I tell you, Marvin *worse* when him brother around. Make poor Clyde suffer too. But May, she not let Clyde take the brunt of it. Some say she spoiled Clyde, but not me. I think she just protected him. But what if she did spoil him, poor soul? He was her only pleasure." Hannah stopped and took a laundered light handkerchief from her bag. She cried into it, crying at the memory. "Oh poor May, she life one long sacrifice, like Lord Jesus himself. I used to take her piece of pie around some time, so she not have to cook. I say to her: May, me not know how you bear your persecutions. And do you know what she answered me, Miss? She quote Lord Jesus: do not wonder if they persecute you, for did they not persecute me also? Now then! "

"Who did she mean?" I asked. "Did she mean the school persecuted her? And the clinic? Or Marvin himself?"

Hannah looked at me, and I saw her realise the depth of my ignorance. "No, my dear," she said soothingly, as she put the handkerchief away. "She mean the same as Saint Paul mean. We fight against unseen powers and principalities, against spiritual wickedness in high places."

* * * * *

I met Clyde and Sylvie through work. We were all teachers, nominally. But of the three of us, only Clyde was the real thing: authoritative, original, patient. Looking back, I think some of his success was the result of his being just what was wanted, then and there. He was, as I said, a gift to the multicultural society. I myself was too common a type to have a marked effect, least of all on children in the schools at that time. I was a young white woman of naive good

7

intentions, bohemian appearance, and a Northern accent interlarded with Hackney. London schools were full of us: I kept bumping into versions of myself in the corridors, which is how I met Sylvie. Like me, she was in her probationary year, but she was nearly ten years older, having gone to college as a mature student. She told me, when we became friends, that she had enrolled at the age of twenty-nine in a final attempt to make a go of her life. She was, she said, 'by nature delinquent' and she wished 'to lay some solid foundation through the marshes of her personality'. I saw that she was like me but much, much worse. She was poised between the tragic and the ridiculous; I was not, I was poised merely between success and failure as a teacher.

As a teacher, Sylvie was hopeless. She had no control over any of her classes; her material was too advanced and theoretical for the children, or sometimes, in feverish over compensation, so elementary they were insulted. They got the measure of her in the first week. Her inability was an unspeakable embarrassment to the other teachers: they could not look her in the eye. I found it hard myself at the beginning, but as I got to know her I became more and more interested, and discounted the fact that she was supposed to be a teacher. She was very good looking. She had the kind of looks I just failed to have myself, which ensured I would be either jealous or a little spellbound. She was of medium height (an inch or two shorter than I) and medium build (therefore more curved than I), with skin oilier and more golden than mine, eyes hazel rather than grey, and hair that hung in heavy uncoiled metallic ropes: gold, copper and brass. My hair had the same shine, the same mixed money colours, but not the weight. At school, people often mistook us for each other, for we wore the same kind of velvet-and-rags clothes fashionable at the time, and Sylvie did not look ten years older than me, or indeed any older at all. But Clyde always knew us apart.

Clyde treated me - at the beginning, anyway - with the same courteous correctness he showed the other white teachers. When I knew him I saw that he dealt with white people by humouring them, as one does lunatics and unsafe animals. There was the distance, the superficial agreement, the guardedness, the loathing. But towards Sylvie he was different. Like the children, he had her measure in the first week. It was as if he knew her already, as if he knew something about her. She too, looking up at him that first day, from where she sat in half-light, half-shadow, beside the staff room window, one thigh negligently crossed over the other, reminding me of a certain French film star, she too seemed to recognize him. A long time later, when it was over and she was in her misery, going over it all obsessionally, I asked her what it was she had recognized. "He was what was going to happen next," she said. "You can always tell." So they did not smile, either of them, because, at the level where they would engage, they already knew each other.

Clyde was sparing of his smiles generally. When, later, I heard people describe Marvin as sulky, I recognized some family likeness in Clyde. But his parsimony with smiling, his holding back of response, was one of the things that made him a good teacher. Unlike the rest of us, he did not court popularity with the children. He did not care whether they liked him, he cared whether they learned to read and write. He believed - it was heresy at the time, but that counted for nothing with him - that he knew a great deal more than his pupils, and that he was there to transmit his knowledge to them. It went without saying that one of the things he must transmit was the expertise of learning: how to use all available means to educate oneself. He told me this once - and I mean once, for he never repeated himself needlessly - he told it laconically, and went on to say he had never been able to see the point of rival educational philosophies.

"Did you ever ask him for help?" I said to Sylvie one day, towards the end of the misery. "With your teaching?"

She nodded. "A couple of times. It was no use. I believed the same as he did already, I tried to act the same, but it didn't work with me. The kids could see through it." She rubbed her eyes wearily and reached for a cigarette. "I've come to the conclusion it was because of his brother. That he was good at teaching. He knew before he started what wouldn't work."

I lit up too. "What is it with Marvin, anyway? What's the matter with him?"

She breathed out smoke and rested her cheek on her hand, staring unfocused into the middle distance. "Who knows? He's what the Yanks call 'mean'. You know he nearly killed…her?"

All I knew was that 'her' was Donna, a black girl Clyde now loved, the girl for whom he had left Sylvie.

"No, I didn't! When?"

"The night of the party. I thought I'd told you all about it."

"You told me there was some trouble, a fight or something, and Clyde took Donna home afterwards. You never told me in detail."

"No, well, that wasn't the part that… Oh, I don't know that I want to go over it all again. I don't want to keep remembering him in detail." She wept anew, face in her hands.

I held her in my arms. "It doesn't matter. "

She was still dangerously frail; I worried about her, as if she were ten years younger, rather than older than me. She was not able to conceal herself. Everyone at the school had known about the affair between her and Clyde, the love affair. She had not told anyone about it, not in words (needless to say, he had not), but her actions, her helpless reactions, blazoned it everywhere. Even the children knew. Their attitude towards her shifted: they half admired, half jeered at her. They obeyed her orders sometimes, sniggering and signaling to each other even before her back was turned. She tried to keep her emotions unobserved, knowing that was the right thing, the thing other people did, even, God help us, the thing men like; but she was not able to, they were too big. Clyde affected not to notice. We were all used to covering up our embarrassment about Sylvie.

As time went by, though, I observed (since I watched them closely, being their friend) hints of amusement in the swift, intent glances Clyde threw her from time to time. Later, the hints were of indulgence, even pity. With the passage of months Sylvie became muted, some weary emotion started to show. When Clyde looked at her now, he held his gaze for longer, but it was not ardent. The right side of his top lip would lift a fraction, in the embryo of a sneer. I guessed then that it was only a matter of time.

During that love affair I did not see much of them, except at school, and I was glad. My own life was hard, and needed all my attention. I was learning how to be a teacher, and I did learn, but I also learned, as one painful day succeeded another, that I would never be really good at it. I had no knack with children, everything was trial and error, everything. Certain of my lessons would be runaway successes, with all the children attentive and hardworking, not wanting to finish when the bell rang. Others, prepared with equal care and imagination, would not even reach the starting gate, the class would be pandemonium. I would scrupulously analyse each factor, as I had been taught at college, but I never reached an unequivocal answer about anything. This incomprehension made me miserable, and I was glad when the end of the school year approached. I did notice, through my preoccupation, that Sylvie was away from school more than usual. She suffered from skin rashes, migraines and stomach upsets regularly, which kept her away for a week at a time. At the beginning of the love affair she had been unusually well, then, one by one, her psychosomatic troubles had started to come back. Now it seemed we had been covering her classes, or getting supply staff in, for many weeks. She had not written or telephoned the school. Finally the Head asked Clyde.

"Couldn't say," he replied silkily. "I haven't seen her myself for a while."

He would say little more to me, except to guess that she was still living in the same place, her flat in Newington Green. "She comes round to my house some nights and stands outside. It's crazy! Just stands there for maybe half an hour, looking at the window in the door. I wish she wouldn't. It upsets Marvin. I have to stop him going out to her. Maybe if you see her you could tell her not to."

"What happened between you, Clyde?" I hardly dared ask, he had become so standoffish. His friendship with me had, after all, been as brief as his affair with Sylvie.

He shrugged. "What usually happens." He sneered a little. "I don't think I was her first young love, who broke her heart. There's no big story. I wouldn't have the time to tell it, even if there were. I have to take three classes now, altogether, in the hall. Work is what matters."

He was hard-hearted, but his life had been hard. Ever since his mother had died, he had had to support his useless, violent brother. Work mattered more to him than to most: he had always had dependants. I wanted to hate him for making my friend unhappy, but I couldn't.

That evening I went to Sylvie's flat. She was in; I had only half expected her to be. She was ashamed to ask me in, but I went in all the same. It was untidy and neglected, and so was she. Her hair was like tarred rope; empty wine bottles and cigarette packets lay here and there; a teapot full of cold tea stood on the table, and next to it a half-eaten sandwich on a paper bag. She sat down passively and allowed me to make fresh tea and some toast. Then she told me that it was over between her and Clyde, that it had finally finished at a party some time ago where he had met someone else. The new person was a black girl, younger than Sylvie, who was in some way political.

"He says she has backbone." she winced as she told it. "He says I'm formless, all over the place. He's right.

I can't make a success of anything. I don't even know how to try."

I said the usual comforting, bracing things, but she was too acute in her insights. It made me uncomfortable, even panicky. I wished I had not taken her on as a friend. She looked levelly at me and asked if I would spend the summer holidays with her, until she got back on her feet. I couldn't; I felt I would sink with her if I went any deeper into her life. So I made excuses, wretchedly, and, in the way she forgave me, saying it was alright and I was not to worry, I felt her age and my own youth for the first time.

I should like to be able to say I thought about her all that summer, visited her often, or at least feared for her, but I did none of those things. It was a summer of enormous relief for me; relief that my probationary year was over, that I could earn my living teaching if I wished, relief that I did not have to, because I was young and had other gifts. Relief, too, that I was away from them all, Clyde, Sylvie, the school and all its problems. I need not have anything further to do with any of it! I travelled.

And then the summer ended and I came back, and I had not looked for another job. So there I was at the same school, there was Clyde, there were the others. So then I thought about Sylvie again, and again went to see her. She was looking low, and older, but she had not killed herself. She was moving towards the end of her misery. She was pleased to see me, wanted to hear about my travels, compared them with her own when young (her words) and washed her hair.

In the days that followed, as she pulled herself together, Sylvie told me Clyde and Marvin's story, which had been her own for a few months.

"He was never completely with me. Not a hundred percent. He always had to think about his brother. Ever since the mother died, Marvin was Clyde's responsibility. It got in the way of everything. It was like having a child that never grew up."

I asked what was the matter with Marvin - medically, officially the matter. Was he simple minded? Was he autistic? Was he delinquent? Was he just a nasty piece of work - officially a 'psychopathic personality'?

She sighed. "All of them. He has never been labelled officially. Labelling is out, you're not supposed to do it, you know."

"Well, did he go to a special school? Or whatever non-label they're called now?"

She shook her head. "May tried to get him into one - that was the mother - because he wasn't learning anything at school. When he was about nine or ten, I think. But they told her they couldn't take him because there were already too many black children there."

"But that's discrimination!"

"No, they seemed to think it was 'anti-discrimination'. I don't know how they worked it out, but they did. And of course it left May to cope with him. But at least he loved her, spasmodically. Clyde says he did. But he hates Clyde. And now Clyde's landed with him. I wanted Clyde to leave him." Her face lit up and darkened with memory. "I wanted the two of us to leave London, secretly. I wanted us to go to Scotland. We were going to drive up there in one night, tell nobody; and start a new life. The Social Services would have had to step in and see to Marvin then."

"Why didn't you?" But I knew. It was the kind of thing you talk about, late at night; but not the kind of thing you do. Her shoulders lifted and lowered. She looked beautiful and ruined, like a city after a war.

"He seemed keen at first. But he always felt guilty about the idea. Sometimes he was hostile towards me for not understanding that. I think he despised me for it. Whereas with her..." She turned away before resuming. "She, this new one, Donna, she thought she could help Marvin. Oh, he loved her for that! She couldn't help him, as it turned out, but it didn't matter. He loved her for wanting to. She's even gone to live with the two of them, even after Marvin tried to strangle her!"

"Marvin what?!"

"Tried to strangle her. At a party. He nearly did it too. I was there."

"Good God, Sylvie, I can't believe this." She merely shrugged again, so I went on. "Why isn't he behind bars? What did the police do?"

17

"There weren't any police. Donna herself didn't want them called. I mean after she came round. She just wanted to go home. So we took her home. Clyde and me. We stayed with her. Only. . ." she looked at me with defeated eyes and a smile of endurance. "By morning it was Clyde with her and me out in the cold."

"But surely not the very…"

"No, no, they didn't get into bed together. She went to sleep on the sofa. Clyde lay down on the floor beside her, in front of the gas fire. He kept turning it down because he was too hot, and then up again because he thought she was cold. I sat on a chair. In the end I went into Donna's bed in the next room. I thought he would come too. But…" She shook her head, and turned so I would not see her face. "The next morning they were still lying as I had left them, only closer. They were both asleep. So I left." I made to embrace her, but she smiled and stepped away. "It's all right now. It's beginning to feel like the past. In a queer way I'm beginning to be glad I'm out of it. I don't think things are too good between them now, anyway."

I sat down again, trying to take it all in. "What happened to Marvin that night?" I asked finally. "Who sorted him out? How did it all start?"

"It started because Donna's political." She talked, making tea and sandwiches for us. As Sylvie moved about I was glad; she was beyond just sitting, crying and smoking; she would recover. "Clyde knew her by sight already, but didn't like her. She was always lecturing him about how he should treat Marvin. "Include Marvin in his success" was what she said. She's the secretary of that group that meets at the Readers' and Writers' Co-operative. New Black Society. They know everything about everybody, so it seems. Clyde didn't like that. He used to say the whole lot of them were a pain in the ass."

"So what changed his mind?"

"I think it was because she had guts. She didn't just talk, tell other people how to live. She took Marvin on herself. At that party, she took him with her upstairs somewhere to talk to him, raise his consciousness. I know it sounds ridiculous -" she saw my expression, " - but that's what she did. She was naive of course, like all these people. But at least she put herself in the front line."

"You sound as if you've fallen for her yourself."

"I do admire her, yes. Even though she's wrong, and anyone could see she was wrong all along. Coming to a blues party with a sheaf of political leaflets - I ask you!"

"Good God! Like the Salvation Army - "

"I know! But sometimes you can't help admiring them either."

"So what happened?"

"Well, needless to say, Marvin didn't want his consciousness raised, he didn't know what she was talking about, he thought she was from the police - this all came out afterwards - but then he made a grab for her, up there in that bathroom. He was liable to do that with women; Clyde had to see he wasn't left alone with women." She bit a sandwich abstractedly. I frowned into my tea. How little I knew about anybody.

"And then he tried to strangle her?"

"No, not then. He wanted the other thing just then. But Donna panicked and ran down the stairs and dropped all the leaflets. They went everywhere. He followed her and slipped on them, they were all down the stairs. That made him mad. It was Errol who told us all this. He was standing in the hall with some people, he was facing the stairs, and saw it all, Donna run down, the papers fall, Marvin run down, Marvin fall."

I sniggered, "I'm sorry Sylvie, but it sounds like bad slapstick."

"I know, but it turned nasty right then. He reached her just as she was coming into the room, and that's when he did it."

She drank from her cup, all misery gone in the engrossment of what she was telling me. "It seemed ages before anyone knew what was happening. The room was jammed solid, the noise was like it always is. Josh had had new amplifiers installed that day, so it was louder than ever. Anyway, I saw somebody's fist go" - she smacked her own against the palm of her hand - "and then there was a space in the crowd and I saw some people on the floor. There was Marvin and two men holding him. There was Donna lying still. I thought she was dead. It was weird, like a dream. And all the time that song pounding away from the amplifiers."

"What song?"

"You never leave him," she said. "That's the name of the song," she said impatiently. She sang a few bars to remind me, but I had never heard the song. "You never leave him, You love him too much," she sang.

I shook my head.

She looked at me, nonplussed. "That's funny. I thought I'd played it to you. It must have been…anyway, never mind."

So she didn't even know who I was, beyond being one of the female admirers I guessed she could always depend on having, wherever life took her.

"That song," she said. "I used to say it described how I was about Clyde and how Clyde was about his brother. He didn't like that. I think it hurt him because it was true."

I got up to leave. "So are they all living together now? Clyde never talks to me these days. Not since you and he…finished. I don't get asked to parties or anything."

"I don't think he goes to any himself. She makes him go to meetings instead. I've heard they're not happy."

"How did you hear?"

"From Josh. I'm seeing quite a bit of him these days."

"Ah." Josh was a local 'operator', a saggerman, a sort of man I had not known existed until I lived in Stoke Newington. He was not a crook, not full-time anyway. But neither, despite his owning of small clubs and buying up of derelict houses, was he a full-time entrepreneur. He blended legal with illegal, in ways the city police knew all about and I knew nothing about. He was in fact a black version of the East End 'wide boys', about whom I also knew nothing. I had been to his blues parties with Clyde and Sylvie. I had felt out of my depth with him, one minute in awe, the next repelled, but all the time aware of being sized up in turn. I suddenly saw how likely it had been, all along, that he and Sylvie should drift together.

"Watch your step with him," I said as I left, just as if I were as sophisticated as herself.

She smiled. "There's no danger. I know where I am with Josh. He lays it on the line. I don't love him, but he's so, oh, after Clyde, and Marvin, and all that scene .... such a relief."

On the doorstep she said. "Come and see us. If I move in with him, that is. I might."

"Where does he live?"

"De Beauvoir."

I said I probably would, some time, but knew I would not. We hesitated. I felt like kissing her goodbye. In fact it was she who gave the kiss, startling me. "You're a better person than I am," she said. "You think I'm glamorous, but you'll amount to more in the long run."

I went away pleased and hurt: a younger sister praised for being clever by an older one who had no need to be.

* * * * *

I worked on at the school and became more used to teaching. I was never good at it, but I was no worse than most. I began to accept the ordinariness of it, and of myself. A diffuse sadness took root in me and became permanent.

I saw Clyde only as one teacher sees another; as a familiar figure in the staffroom and in assembly, one among many. Then one day came news of his impending resignation. It was said he intended emigrating to The Sahel. The Head tried to persuade him to stay. The school secretary overheard some of the argument. Clyde said, it seemed, that he felt a black teacher had no business teaching white children when there were so many black children in the world not being taught.

"But white children need black teachers too," said the Head, "to combat racism."

Clyde replied, "Black children need them more, for more urgent reasons."

The Head said "But how will we fill our quota?" and Clyde said "What is that to me?"

We others talked about it in the staffroom, but not to Clyde himself. He was no longer sociable. He had been standoffish for a long time now; ever since, I calculated, he had lived with Donna. I was full of curiosity about them all; they seemed symbolic in some way, crucial to my understanding of life. Shortly after Clyde's talk with the Head we read in the Hackney Gazette that Marvin had been arrested. It was front-page news. He had taken Clyde's car and driven it without a licence, had collided head-on with another car, killing the driver and injuring himself in the chest. There were many witnesses. Clyde was angry when he saw us around the paper. He would say nothing. The case re-entered the 'Gazette' for Marvin's trial: a photograph showed him still bandaged. Clyde was away from school that day, testifying, so we could talk freely. It was thought Marvin would be ordered to a Detention Centre, and be fined as well. "Which will mean Clyde pays", said Margaret Shaw, Head of the Remedial Department. Charlie Hampden, the Deputy Head, pressed his lips together and shook his head. "It won't be just the fine that Clyde will have to stand. If you ask me, the Social Services Department, and the National Health Psychiatrists Department or whatever, will put in a plea for a short sentence so long as he's released into the care of a responsible relative."

"In other words, Clyde."

"Of course."

"So Clyde can say goodbye to the Sahel."

"Or to anywhere else outside of N16 for the next few years."

"What was he going to do with his brother anyway? If he emigrated?"

People shrugged. "Leave him to his fate."

"He wouldn't," I said. "Clyde would never leave him."

"Well, I don't know," said Barry Robertson, huffily. "You were the one who knew him best. What *did* he intend on doing with the brother?"

I did not know. "I don't know, but I should think he'd take him with him."

"He'd be a fool if he did," said Charlie. "From what I've seen, and heard of that brother, he's backward and vicious. Clyde should have taken any way out he could from being stuck with him."

I thought of Sylvie and her plan to rescue Clyde and escape to Scotland.

"But he is his brother, after all,'" said Jim Virdee, a Sikh teacher who took boys' games and also operated loop-films, slide-lanterns and the like.

"That's no reason for him to carry him on his back all his life," said Barry.

"But it is," said Jim.

* * * * *

What Charlie had predicted, happened. Clyde was to undertake full legal responsibility for his brother as soon as Marvin had served three months' detention. Nothing was said in the paper about who was to pay Marvin's fine; since there was no-one else to pay it, Clyde must have paid.

"Paying the fine for having his own car smashed," said Barry. "He'll have to pay for a new car as well. And now he's got to look after the bastard for the rest of his life. It's a funny sort of justice.

"It's fate," said Jim Virdee. "It's hard, yes, but not everything can be made easy."

No more was heard about Clyde's resignation. He continued at the school, stiff and reserved in the staffroom, rebuffing sympathy, rebuffing conversation altogether, yet patient with the children, still a good teacher.

I wondered and wondered about him and his new girl. I could not imagine what sort of life they must have, after what Sylvie had told me. The thought that a woman could move in with the brother of someone who had tried to kill her; the thought that Clyde could let the man who had attacked her live with them - I could make no sense of it. If they had been illiterate heavy drinkers, fighting one night and swearing devotion the next, it would have been recognizable. The only other pattern that would hold the parts was a religious one - Clyde and the girl were saints. If that were true, they would get their martyrdom all right, in the years that lay ahead. I shuddered to think of it, to think that Clyde must lose his lively brilliance - indeed he had closed that off already - his good humour, his wit, strength, even, eventually, his looks, that all might become grist to the mill of endurance. It was repellant, I looked away, turned in relief to other people.

* * * * *

There was a man who spent his days among the streets of Stoke Newington, playing a flute. He was as familiar as the gangs of rude-boys who jigged and stamped at every corner, but he was very different. Crook-backed and not young, he nursed his flute like a pet bird, drawing from it pale, formless tunes that haunted the brain. Like the rude-boys he was black, but they drew away from him as from an alien. No-one said "Hey, man!" His hair, long and rough, rattled about his bony shoulders in plaits, or ringlets. We did not yet have the word 'dreadlocks', so no word could quite describe them. He wore a tunic of patches, at once ragged and showy, and Indian sandals on his bare feet.

Sylvie and I used to wonder about him, idly and happily, during the time she was with Clyde ... Sylvie was reminded of an ascetic from the early church.

"He spoke to me once," she said. "When he smiled I saw his teeth. They're filed to points."

I was scared and interested. "What did he say?"

"He said 'The Lion of Judah shall break every chain'. Just that."

"And then what?"

"Nothing. He turned his mouth back to the flute and shuffled along the pavement in those sandals."

She had asked Clyde about him, but he knew nothing.

But Josh knew, because Josh always had the latest news from Jamaica. He told us one day about the man with the flute. We met by chance at his Camleigh Road house, where he held the blues parties. We, that is Sylvie, Clyde and I, had gone to pick up Marvin who did odd jobs for Josh. We ended in Josh's private sitting room, around a low, heavy glass coffee-table, drinking whisky.

"It goin' big over there," Josh told us. "Marcus Garvey's religion. Call it Rastafari, African word. It all about goin' back to Africa. It soon be here, you see. That man just the first." Idly he rolled a set of poker-dice on the glass table-top.

"We guessed it was a religion of some kind," I said. "What is it, then? Black Muslims? Voodoo? Something Jewish?"

"Why you say that?"

"Well…Judah. He said 'The Lion of Judah' to Sylvie. Judah's Jewish."

He shrugged. "I don't know, girl. Bits of this, bits of that. They think the Emperor of Ethiopa goin' to send some golden ships for them." He laughed silently. "*He* the Lion of Judah. The Emperor of Ethiopia."

"Haile Selassie? Are they serious?"

"Who knows? Maybe they're right. They think so anyway."

"But, golden ships!" This was Clyde. "When are they supposed to be coming?"

"They come when they come. That give them all excuse not to go catch a plane to Africa, if that's where they want to go." He altered his voice to a whine, a parody. "Them sit here in Babylon waitin' for them golden ships."

"Babylon! Why Babylon? They're not in captivity."

Josh rolled the dice, picked them up, rolled them again.

"Everywhere Babylon to them," he sneered. "Everywhere captivity. Jamaica, Babylon, England, Babylon, USA, Babylon. They just wait an' suffer, waitin' for the golden ships."

"Them golden ships," Marvin spoke, startling all of us, even Josh. He so rarely spoke, and only when badgered with questions, that it was a shock to hear his voice spontaneously. He could not control the tones, which slid from a whine to a hoarse shout. "I want to go see them ships! I want to *see* them golden ships! Them golden ships on the seven seas."

We were all silent, then Clyde recovered himself. "I'll take you on a ship. We'll go on a trip somewhere."

Marvin turned quickly, snarling. "Not with you, man! Not your fuckin' ship!" He was squeaking with rage. Tears stood in his eyes, he got up and made for the door.

"Hey, Marvin!" Josh was as used to him as Clyde was. "Hey, Marvin! You do me a favour, I give you a ten! That's real! Now then, you find Errol, get him to show you how to watch doors and windows. I got a new girl working, 'cross the street. I can't watch all the time, I got other things to do. Get Errol to show you how to check each time anybody go in there, come out there. Anybody who'd be paying."

Marvin turned; he was listening intelligently. "You give me a ten for that?"

"A ten if you get it right! Nothing if you don't. You get Errol to show you how."

"I go now?"

"Sure. You find him in the back kitchen."

Considering, Marvin opened the door and reluctantly went out. Immediately Josh rang Errol on the internal phone and told him what to expect. Not for the first time, I marvelled at the ease with which he managed Clyde's brother.

Clyde's face was hidden, his fingers pressed against his forehead in a way that looked habitual. After a moment he dropped his hands, sighed, and lit a cigarette.

"How do you know all this?" he asked, coldly, it seemed to me. "About the new religion and the golden ships? And what's the flute- player got to do with it?"

Josh did not answer immediately. Half-smiling, he stared at Clyde. The beginning of a laugh rose to his lips.

"What kind of question that, man? How do I know? I know a lot more things than you. You know I know a lot more things than you. I understand that fuckin' Marvin better than you, don't I? That what hurt, isn't it? That what make you wild?" He sniggered openly, then ostentatiously straightened his face. "Well, Clyde, to answer your other question. Some people I know that you *don't* know, just in from Kingston this week, they recognize that man. The one you call the flute-player. They say him Jah's holy disciple. Them was the words they said. We saw him in the street, an' they took their hats off to him. Hats, yes! Green an' yellah an' red, I don't know, I never saw such hats. Made of wool, as if them poor old women. An' all that hair hangin' down below. It big new religion in Kingston, got police there runnin' scared."

"Police scared?" It was I who asked. "Why, if it's a religion?"

He gave me the brief, scornful look I was familiar with.

"Aw, you know, them smoke a lotta weed, go thiefin' to get the money. Make they own laws up, won't do what policeman tell them."

He yawned and stood up, pocketing the dice. "Newspapers there say them destroyin' society. Women all scared their children go join Rasta people, drop outta school, do no work. It comin' here next, is the buzz. That man, that flute-player, him just the first. I gotta go out now. Someone comin' to my other house

31

at six o'clock." He went to the door that led down to the kitchen and called. We heard people coming up, one of them Marvin; Josh talked to them and they went back below.

"I told him he can stay here tonight. With Errol. Can learn the job." He smiled. "Ain't that nice for you, Clyde, hey man? Ain't I do you a good turn? You can have a night off. Go for a long drive somewhere with this sweet lady." He steered the back of his fingers down Sylvie's hair and lightly onto her cheek. I saw her head involuntarily stir, for a moment, towards the fingers.

"Go a long, long way," he murmured, "Scotland or somewhere." Abruptly he dropped his hand and turned. "OK Clyde, keep in touch. Have some more drinks if you want, make yourselves at home. I gotta go." Picking up a cashmere coat, he left.

* * * * *

The next year the followers of Jah appeared on the streets of London, in little groups, or one at a time, and then in numbers. And where they appeared the rude-boys were seen no longer. Perhaps they became followers themselves; perhaps, seeing themselves no longer the newest and youngest, they grew up and became just men; finally, perhaps they acknowledged the spiritual force of the new movement and bowed down before it. The followers of Jah changed everything the young West Indians did: clothes, music, even their food. They began to stand aloof from whites, aloof from their own parents, whom they saw as collaborators. I, and other white people, began to experience a strange pain of rejection, strange because it was collective and not personal. I and other white people began to see ourselves as 'white people', a racial group instead of the unique individual souls we were used to. We could do nothing right, for the wrongness was in our colour and in our history, over which we had no control. Cosmopolitan life, the magic cultural alchemy that had drawn me to London, faltered and disconnected, finally broke up into strident separate parts.

I would leave in the summer, I decided, at the end of the school year. I suddenly had no close friends, no inspiration in my work. The growing hostility of public places, where I was 'a white person', made me miserable. I used to watch, wistfully, crowds of prettily dressed West Indian women going into their church on Sunday mornings. They brought to mind the Whitsun walks of my childhood. One Sunday, I went in, nervously, wondering if there too I would count only as 'a white person'. But straight away I saw one of my own pupils, Lloyd Delahaye, sitting with his family.

"Miss Hamilton!" he cried before his mother shushed him. But I was beckoned to sit with them, and did.

I went to the church every Sunday after that. It was a temporary hearth and home in a world grown cold-hearted. Nevertheless I did not want to commit myself to it: I was embarrassed by the naive enthusiasm, the confessions of salvation, the pressure to confess and be saved myself. It was very like the Chapels of my childhood; like them, impossible to stay with. Of course Clyde no longer went. I understood perfectly why he no longer did, even whilst commiserating with Doris, on our walks home, whilst she told me about Clyde and Marvin as infants and the sorrows of their mother.

On the last Sunday, Doris approached me before church.

"Oh Miss, such news 'bout Marvin! I just hear last night, hardly took it in myself yet." Her hands were up at her face, troubled. She paused and looked at me, as if remembering something. "You knew Clyde! Did he ever tell you 'bout Marvin join the Rasta people?"

"Marvin? No, I didn't know. Mind you, Clyde has not talked to me much this past year. And of course I don't see him now."

"No." She nodded. "Nobody see him now. But Marvin, seems he join the Rasta people a while back, John don't know exactly when. Marvin got caught sellin' ganja, went to prison. Oh Miss, if only the young men would leave them things alone! Ganja and strong drink an' all those other evil things! Anyway, another man got sent in same time. That man you maybe seen on streets. Look like a tramp, a bit simple if you want my opinion. Playin' music, an' him teeth all to points like a heathen."

"Oh yes!" And I remembered, I had not seen the flute-player for a long time.

"Disgrace, Miss! Hair hangin' down at his age! An' him from Jamaica! I can't imagine what happenin' in Jamaica now, with this Rasta religion. Jesus said 'No man cometh to the Father but by me.'"

"What happened to Marvin and the other man? You were telling me."

"That right. Well now, in prison they have them workshops. Handicraft an' things. So that man and Marvin ask for wood and nails, that man draw a plan, an' you know what them start to make?"

"What?"

"A boat! Yes, Miss, a boat, an' not a toy boat. A real one. Other prisoners help them. All get enthusiastic, singin' in the workshop, so John say." Her eyes shone, she looked for a moment as if she would join in herself. "Them guards stand there, mouth open, no trouble with any prisoners who make that boat. Anyway, that man have him time cut short for good behaviour, him leave, take the boat with him, half-finished. Marvin has time cut short too. Next thing John hear, the two of them has the boat finished an' floatin' on the River Lee!"

"No!"

"Oh yes, Miss! Hard to believe, I know, but it there. All the children go over there to see it. Hackney

Marshes. Them give them rides. The children say they all goin' to Africa one day."

It was time to go into church; the first notes of the harmonium peeled out. During the service I was shaken with emotions I could not account for. It did not matter; people cried and shouted for joy all the time in that church.

When I saw Doris afterwards there were shining tracks of tears on her cheeks too. We embraced each other, too choked to speak, in the thronged porch.

Looking back, I think the direct bliss of that moment was another reason I could not stay. I could not have borne to watch that rapturous fellowship become ordinary, to descend to tedious weekly chat, and die slowly in a jangle of imitation and boredom.

"You goin' away?" she asked, when we drew apart and started down the steps.

"Yes, I'm going back North. My mother and father are getting old." It was a lie I knew Doris would like; I had chosen it for her. There was nobody, ever, to whom I could tell the truth; and that, I suppose, is the reason for my lifelong loneliness. The best I can do is give people the lies I hope they will like.

"I'd like to have seen Clyde one last time" I said. "I wonder what he makes of Marvin's new life."

"Indeed, Miss, yes! Good coming out of bad like that! See, them Rastas cannot be all bad, by their fruits ye shall know them. And yet I hear bad things too." Her face folded in disappointment as she remembered.

"Some them young men bein' used. Used, I say. Them not choose it. Them bein' used to bring evil things into this country. Into Jamaica as well. Not ganja, I talkin' bout, though me myself get rid of ganja too, all the lot! But this bad stuff Miss, cocaine an' stuff. It ruin Jamaica, you mark my words! Somebody usin' them young men to make some bad man fortune. It come here too Miss, you see." She sounded as overworked by disappointment as I had thought only myself to be. I embraced her again, there in the street. We stood like worn-out horses, heads on each other's necks.

"Never mind," she sighed, lifting hers. "Our Lord himself had to go through the valley of the shadow. Come, walk a bit, my dear. You askin' about Clyde. I thought you knew. Him goin' abroad, now Marvin livin' with the Rastas. Him goin' to Africa, an' that girl too. Maybe some good will come of it. Maybe good will come of all we do. You go look after you Mammy and Daddy, and maybe some time we meet again."

I put my hands to my face and cried. It was too much. I knew that if I stayed, and got to know her well, I would find her full of spite and jealousy and condemnation; as she would find me a liar to the bone. But the moments, like this one, when it was not so! Those transfigurations are all I live for.

I dried my eyes and pretended to cheer up. We had reached Camleigh Road, where our ways parted.

"I'll write," I said, smiling, but this she recognized as a fiction, I am sure. She simply smiled herself and crossed the road and began to walk down the street, looking back to wave from time to time. I stood motionless, watching her go. Turning at the end, she blew me a kiss, her white glove saluting.

I was alone again.

* * * * *

Part Two

I left without ever meeting Donna. I had only Sylvie's description of her, plus one sighting - and perhaps it was someone else: driven by curiosity but shy of making acquaintance, I had hung around the Readers' and Writers' bookshop for an hour one day. But she had taken hold of my imagination, as had Clyde and his brother. I began conjuring up scenes of their life together - Clyde's and Marvin's, and later Donna's - repeatedly, long after I had left the real scene.

I imagined Marvin returning home at dawn, having been out all night, and Clyde going through the motions of being angry with him. He felt not angry but sick, sick of his brother, sick of the responsibility. He had promised their mother he would keep Marvin out of trouble. He saw with chagrin how this promise, part of his identity as a good son, good scholar, good citizen, had shackled him for life. Bad sons, bad citizens, were not asked to keep each other out of trouble. They were applauded if they stayed out of it themselves.

So, going through the motions, he said, "Where you been, Marvin? Where d'you get all that money?"

Marvin had pulled from his pockets a flutter of twenty-pound notes. He was frowning at them, then his face cleared, he almost smiled and pocketed them again.

"Marvin! You hear me! Where d'you get that money?"

"Earnt it." His face closed again.

"Earned it? How? Doing what?"

"None of your business. I goin' to bed now."

"You not goin' to bed till you tell me where you got that money! It *is* my business if you got police after you."

Marvin's mouth twisted. "No police," he sneered. "Josh knows what he doin'."

"You got the money from Josh? What'd he pay you for? What'd you do for him?"

"Pick up Guinness bottles." He sniggered.

"Guinness bottles? Why?"

"Aw shut up, I tell you enough." He turned and stared out the window, chewing his lip.

"Look man, why not tell me? I know Josh as well. Josh knows I gotta know."

Marvin looked at him with the contempt born of intimacy. "Josh don't trust you."

"He don't trust me? Why?" But Clyde knew. He was distrusted because he was not an operator, not a saggerman, like Josh himself, not even a follower, nor a contact, hardly ever a customer. Josh and himself were not on the same side.

"Okay, I'll see Josh myself," said Clyde. He went out and down the street to the betting-shop, but Josh was not there. He tried Lightning Records and a couple of houses. Finally he went to the place he should have gone first: Josh's own club, in the basement of a house he owned in Camleigh Road. The door was locked and the windows dark, but Clyde kept on knocking until the chain was drawn on the inside and he was let in. He found Josh in the back room playing poker. Clyde knew the faces of the three other players, but not their names.

"What a surprise, man," said Josh, not looking up.

"Josh, can I see you a minute?"

"Not really, man, I like this game. Talk to me while we play. If it's worth listening to, I'll listen."

"All right. Why you give Marvin all that money for picking up old Guinness bottles?"

"Oh that." Josh was amused. "Yeah. That kid a good worker. Got me five hundred bottles, must be. Yeah, he earn his money, he not rob me." The glance he gave his cards was casual. "I play these."

"Come on, man. Kids could have done that for ice-cream. Why'd you pay Marvin?"

Josh pushed a twenty-pound note to the stake and said, "He did more than a kid could. See now - he got bottles with labels still on them and found the tops as well. See?"

Clyde understood. The bottles would be filled with fake liquor and sold at the club to new arrivals from

Jamaica, at any price Josh cared to think of. He should have left then. He had found out what he had come to find out. But for some reason he said, "You know the politicals are coming to your club, Saturday?"

Josh's wrist drooped ostentatiously with its five-card fan. His nostrils flared. He pushed another note across the table. "What you talkin' about now, man?"

"That political group, New Black Society. They aim to go round all the clubs; they want everybody to go straight with each other. They won't like your Guinness." But he was half-hearted. All his resistance, his pugnacity, was used up on Marvin. He could not launch himself against anyone else.

Two of the players had thrown in; there was to be a show between Josh and the other. This one now put over two notes and called. Josh turned his hand, displaying a running flush of diamonds. The other man's face slackened. He laid down his full house that had lost. Josh pulled his winnings over, then turned on Clyde like a race-horse still full of mettle. "Now what you want man? You tellin' me about New Black Society; I not interested. I not interested what they think or where they goin'. What you tell me this for, you one of them?"

"No, but the drinks you sell —"

Josh swung about to face him. "Look, man, if the politicals not like my drinks they not drink them. What else can they do? And if I not like *them*, they leave. That go for you too." He pointed an intense finger at

Clyde. "I give people a party, they pay for crap drinks, they not know the difference, they have a good time. If they do know the difference, they learnin'. An' I tell you what they learn, they learn this - you can be a winner if you want to. That what your brother learn from me. That why I more use to him than you." He stripped a note from his winnings. "Here, give him this for keeping his mouth shut, - not too far open anyway." Abruptly he laughed and relaxed. As Clyde made his way out he heard the card-players joining in the laughter.

The next morning, Saturday, Clyde was in Dalston, in the bookshop run by the Readers' and Writers Co-operative. He had left Marvin at home, lying on his bed with a pile of girlie magazines. Clyde often came to this bookshop, and once he had been to the rooms above it that were used for the meetings of the New Black Society. He was not a member of the group. Political talk embarrassed him deeply. It reminded him of the bright sloganizing of his mother's church friends. He couldn't believe anybody could talk that way and mean it. But he was badgered into buying the Group's paper occasionally. It was sold, aggressively, at the school where he taught, and, more and more nowadays, from door-to--door.

As he stood looking at new paperbacks he saw Donna MacIntyre coming down the stairs from the top rooms. She was a member of the New Black Society. She was an intelligent girl, serious to the point of rancour and that was how she liked it. Unfortunately she looked like a pin-up, and this made her angry. One way and another she was angry most of the time. Clyde felt momentarily guilty. He was idling through books whilst she, clearly, had been cyclostyling leaflets. She was carrying a swatch of them. As she caught sight of him she cast him a severe look: she remembered him, too, from his one abortive attendance. Clyde felt cornered: suppose she started to press him to come to another meeting! He had to forestall her. He smiled his handsome smile and began to talk. He talked about Marvin, giving Marvin as the reason he couldn't get out much. But as he elaborated his familiar theme he saw her frown deepen, and guessed with sinking heart that she was subjecting his words to political analysis.

"Your brother's problem is all of our problem," she said. She tucked the leaflets into her shoulder-bag and made for the door. Clyde felt compelled to go with her.

"How do you mean?" he asked. They were out of the shop and walking along the street.

"We should *all* be the bad black man in the eyes of those who have the power. You do no good to point out the difference between him and you. That what the power-holders want: good blacks and bad blacks. With the good ones doing what they're told: keeping the bad ones down. You're Uncle Tom, man."

Clyde was stung into serious argument.

"You said that once before. You say that I reject him and all things bad and black along with him. But remember, I live with him. I always lived with him. I don't reject him, I take him. I'm the one that take what that kid dishes out!" He was angry and enthusiastic. "Your phrases like 'holders of power' and 'Uncle Tom' - that just noises, man, that just conversation. The way it is with us, with me and Marvin: sometimes the holders of power matter, sometimes they don't-"

"You saying," Donna cut in, "that living together with Marvin stop you from seeing things politically."

"I saying," said Clyde, "that living together with anybody stop you from seeing them politically. Marvin and me, we just got each other, like it or not."

"Why - like it or not?" Donna was sharp. "You could walk out on him. At least that would be honest."

Clyde stopped walking and faced her, nearly shouting. "What good would my fuckin' honesty do if he got picked up by white police the day after I leave?"

"Why do you care if it does him good or not? You been telling me how he bug you, how he drag you down; how can it matter to you what he feel?"

"He my brother!" shouted Clyde. "I don't know why else I care, I don't know the cause of it!"

Donna looked at him and twisted her lips. "I think he need better than that. If he a drag on you, if he spoil your nice life, leave him. He must know you want to; nobody that stupid. Let the people who really care about him find him."

"People who really care about him? Do you mean New Black Society?"

"That right, I mean us. We are the bad black force: he a bad black man. He belong to us."

"Who are you bad for? Why bad?"

"Bad for whitey, bad for the holders of power. You are a child."

"But Marvin is bad to me, and I'm black. He not political at all!"

"Everyone political, whether they know it or not. As for you - you white somewhere, you know. That why he bad to you."

"You crazy, you talk shit, you know nothing about us!" Clyde stepped away from her, repelled. "He was bad to my mother, he would be bad to you if he could! And you say it prove we all secret whites if Marvin is bad to us! You talk shit!"

He turned away and left her standing on the street, her head thrust out, one hand on her hip, animated with hostility.

* * * * *

Josh's club was in a house he owned in Camleigh Road, a short walk from the street where Clyde and Marvin lived. Camleigh Road had been built for cheap splendour in the nineteenth century and had now decayed into furnished rooms. The basement of Josh's house had been converted into the club; he let the upper floors to old Irishmen and despairing white couples with babies. At the moment Josh's long, pale car was parked in front of the house. The club would be open in a few hours. He had come to see the installing of the amplifiers but the van had not arrived. Josh sipped whisky while he waited, and frowned. He had just seen that the clock on the wall behind the bar had been smashed. He opened a door beside the bar. "Errol, come here!"

At the end of the passage a man looked out, holding a glass and a tea-cloth.

"Come here, Errol. Look at this." Josh ushered him and pointed to the smashed clock. "Who done that?"

Errol's eyes widened. "Oh, that what it was! That must have been Marvin, boss. He was in here this afternoon. I hear a noise like something break, I thought he break a glass. When I got in here he gone and I don't see nothing."

"Uh-huh. O.K. Get this cleared up, huh? I don't want them walking on glass when they bring the boxes in."

Errol retreated, to reappear with brush and shovel. Josh had folded back the shutters and was staring out of the window. "Where those bastards get to?" he mused. It was always a hassle getting the amplifiers to the right place at the right time. But it was better than installing sets in all his clubs; it cost less money.

Suddenly remembering, he went out to the kitchen to count the crates of fake Guinness. They were well-packed, professional- looking. A year ago he had bought up a small firm that made soft drinks for the

47

West Indian market. It had been an easy deal. The owners, two old men, had had no idea how to do business. Josh had had a hunch that the little firm with its bottling plant would be useful to him some day. The bar was stocked with job-lots of cheap wine and rum; in a concealed safe in the kitchen Josh kept good whisky for himself and the men he would do business with that night.

There was knocking on the outside door. "Open the door, Errol. They're here." But when Errol opened the door it was only Marvin who came in.

"What you want, Marvin?" Josh was vexed. "I expecting the van with those boxes."

Marvin shrugged his shoulders and went into the main club-room with the tables and the bar. He sat down at a table, propping his head on his hands. Josh followed him in. "Now what you want? I got a lot to see to."

"Nothing to do," muttered Marvin.

"Wait a minute," Josh remembered. "I got a bone to pick with you. Errol tell me you broke that clock"

Marvin looked over to the bare clock-face in the shadows behind the bar, and said nothing.

"Answer me, boy! How did you break my clock?"

"Hit it."

"Hit it? How?"

Marvin curled his fist and crashed it down onto the table so that the ashtray jumped.

"Like that."

Josh looked up at the clock. It had not stopped: the hands were at ten past five, the same as his watch.

"You mean you climbed up there and hit it in the face?"

Marvin's lips twisted, he cast his eyes down.

"You crazy man?" Josh was interested. "What you do a crazy thing like that for? You must be crazy man to hit a clock. Hey - you been drinkin'?"

Errol, standing silently beside the bar, broke in. "He *was* drinkin', boss. He'd his own bottle. I gave him a glass."

At this Marvin shifted, put down one hand and drew from his overcoat pocket a whisky bottle "Can I have a glass?"

Josh was wordless, then he collected himself and nodded to Errol. "Bring one for me too. And one of the flasks from the kitchen. Now, Marvin, tell me why you hit the clock." But as Marvin went on smirking and saying nothing his temper changed. "Now you listen to me, boy! You tell me why you done that crazy thing or you go right out of this club now and I never let you in again! You got me real mad!"

Errol brought the flask of whisky and the two glasses; Josh poured himself a measure and drank it off. "Don't you get me mad, boy! I fix it so *nothing* go right for you, or your brother. Now you tell me why you smash that clock!"

Marvin's face laboured, his fingers curled and uncurled around the empty glass. Finally, "I wanted it to stop." he said.

"You wanted it to stop? Why? Why you want it to stop?"

Again the effort in Marvin's face. "It make too much noise. It spoil everything. I was enjoyin' myself." The clock ticked in the silence. Josh sighed and sat down beside him. "Well that's all right," he said. "What was you doing?"

"Nothing."

Josh took Marvin's whisky bottle and handed it to Errol. As Marvin made to grab it Josh laid hold of him and pushed him back to his seat. "Listen boy, you get no whisky till you stop saying nothing. Now you tell me what you mean you was enjoying yourself. What was you doing?"

"He was drinking, boss," said Errol. "He didn't do nothing else. Not while I was here."

"But you wasn't here all the time, Errol, so shut your mouth. Marvin I talking to you, boy! Answer me!" And as Marvin's face twisted away again Josh hit it as it turned, across the mouth. "Answer me!" He got up and stooped over the boy. "Answer! Answer!"

Marvin rose and tried to push his way out, but Errol stepped forward. They were now both in front of him, one at each side of the table, and the wall at his back.

He sat down and covered his face. "What you want me to say? I was drinkin', I was by myself, I wasn't doing nothin' to nobody! The sun was shinin' round the shutters there; it was like somebody was in this room with me and the sun comin' round the shutters there. Then somebody say "Marvin, you good." It was like-"

"Somebody say that? Who say that?" Josh still stood, overshadowing him.

"Boss, wasn't nobody here but Marvin and me!"

"Shut your mouth, Errol. I know there wasn't nobody else here. Marvin, who said that to you? Was it yourself?"

Marvin groaned. "No. I not know. I forgotten. It was like somebody was in this room with me." His voice broke, he covered his face with his hands.

"All right then," said Josh. "That's all right. Here, take a drink." He poured some from his own flask and pushed the glass gently to Marvin. "Then what happened?"

Marvin shook his head and took the whisky, his heavy hand trembling. The windows rattled; from the street came a slamming of doors. A moment later the club door was opened and voices shouted "Sound system, Mr. Lewis!"

"Tell them to stand right where they are for one minute, Errol, then I come."

As Errol left, Josh asked, "How did it end, Marvin? How you come to hit the clock?"

Marvin swallowed his whisky and turned his face aside again. "That clock make too much noise'" he

51

sneered. "It spoil everything." The clock tick-tocked in the shadows; he had not stopped it, he had only broken the glass.

Josh sighed. He swallowed another drink, then got to his feet. "All right, then. Don't break anything more in this club, you understand? Now come on; you help me get this system switched on."

* * * * *

Donna frowned over two piles of duplicated paper. One was made up of faultless reproductions; the other was a pile of failures: both the ink-sodden and the bald. She frowned because she did not wish to be the sort of woman who could not work machines. She began to staple the good pages to others which made up the second sheet. She was going to take the leaflets to a number of clubs that night, and hand them round personally. Ideally each club would then become a political cell. Donna knew quite well that this would not happen, yet she must work as though it would. She felt sad and isolated, banging away at the stapler. She was not like her comrades. None of them doubted that a well-leafletted club would turn into a cell. Success in politics went to people like that: people who only knew what they believed.

Donna lit a cigarette and read through the leaflet while she smoked, trying to read it as a stranger would. She had written it herself and the rest of the group had not seen it yet. She feared their judgement. If they were to say it was bullshit she would feel sure it was. The men in the group did not like her; her looks irritated them. She looked like a nice easy time but wasn't. She argued and wrote leaflets, she would not keep her mouth shut, she was most definitely not what they wanted. They liked the other girls in the group; girls who were plainer and said less.

Donna was lonely, nobody seemed right for her. She had once, one night only, found her true society. She had gone down to Charing Cross arches on a freezing winter night, with leaflets, to try and make contact with some homeless teenagers she had heard about. She had made contact all right. By the end of the night she was lying with a sixteen-year-old boy, under both their coats, burning under his soft hands, burning in the frost, the pair of them. She had walked all the way home, that dark rigid morning, through all the streets of London, walking away from what she had done. She never brought it to mind now, but it came all the same. The pages lay unstapled, and on to them fell a lump of ash from her guttering cigarette. She stubbed it out and picked up the stapler, working and working until her thoughts were in order again.

* * * * *

Seven o'clock in the evening, and Sylvie was dressing to go to the club with Clyde. They had spent the afternoon in her bed, and now she must leave it. Clyde was in the next room making coffee.

"Clyde!"

"Uh-huh?"

"Will I be the only white one there?"

His laugh sounded startled. "I don't know. Maybe you will. Does it bother you?"

She considered, her silk dress in her hands. "Yes. It looks as if I'm on show."

Clyde brought in two cups of coffee and put them beside her. "Don't you want to be on show?" he mocked. "Beautiful girl like you." But he repented and took her shoulders softly in his hands. "It was good just now," he whispered.

She twisted to face him; her hands stroked his satiny sides. "Let's go away somewhere tonight," she pleaded. "We could drive all night - shall we go to Scotland? Maybe it would rain and be misty in the morning as we crossed the border."

She wove these enchantments sometimes. He felt the pull of it: he wanted to make that journey. He bent his face and kissed her; she drew him down to the bed again.

Afterwards Sylvie was sad. In a hesitant voice, because she was not sure of him, she asked, "Shall we go, then? To Scotland?"

He resented her for making him explain. "No. You know we can't."

She remembered. "Because of Marvin?"

"Yes."

"Why should he rule your life like this?" She was ashamed of complaining and she knew it rubbed Clyde sore to hear her.

"There isn't any 'should' about it." His voice was cold. "It's not that he should or shouldn't rule my life, it's that he does."

"But he's not a baby!" Sylvie burst out. "How is it he can manage sometimes without you? Where is he now for instance?"

"Watching television. There are three programmes in a row that he likes. After that he's going straight to Josh's. We'll see him there."

"Was that why you came here early? Because Marvin was watching television?"

"Yes, that's why -" he altered his words, "that's why I was able to come early. I'd like to come early every time, you know that."

His courtesy snubbed her; she felt naked and embarrassed. She stood up and, turning her back, began to dress. Clyde looked at her white, childish back and felt pity for her. He would never leave Marvin for her sake.

* * * * *

On an autumn evening in North-East London, the sky droops rainy folds. A neon sunset makes rose and fire in the west, but the eastern sky is stained with darkness and has a last bird's call in it. The leaves of the plane trees hang as if dead from blackened twigs. The dusk is still: thin rain has velvetted the scaly plane- bark, and on the lustred pavements leaves lie in drifts. Houses which by day are ragged ruins assume a veiled, Spanish beauty in the half-darkness. Luminous as jewels, curtains are drawn across lighted windows. On one doorstep glitters the crushed ice of broken milk bottles. Dustbins lean in the gateways, the sky's last light making vivid all the white things spilling from them: eggshells, margarine tubs and crumpled paper shine white in the ultra-violet.

One basement door stands open. Josh's club has opened but there is nothing doing yet. Beyond the door a table serves as a barrier, and here Errol is sitting, drinking rum and reading a paperback western. After a while he looks at his watch, and as if on cue, the streetlights come on, altering all the colours and throwing new shadows. He notices something else: a distant crowd of voices. He can hear laughter and a clatter of feet. He goes down the passage to the back of the house where Josh and his friends have a card-game started. "They here boss."

Josh stands up, putting down his card. "Okay you carry on without me," he says to his companions, and goes to the controls of the sound-system.

Down from the street the new arrivals, a week out of Kingston, strangers to each other until they met on the plane, crowd into the club, and the music bursts in their faces like a barrage of homecoming.

* * * * *

Sylvie is not the only white at Josh's shebeen tonight. The black pubs of the neighbourhood all have their white regulars. Failed writers, jumpy with insights the world does not want, can get drunk there unembarrassed, not feeling eccentric or rejected, because they know that to black men all whites look alike. There, too, are confused and exhausted social workers, desperate to pick up insights, though not the ones the writers have on offer. School teachers drink there as part of their effort to belong to the community. All these people get drunk easily: some of them are halfway to alcoholism without recognizing it. And always there are one or two bitterly shy, defeated young men who hope the music and hipness of the blacks will rub off on them. These familiar faces from the pubs have been invited to Josh's along with everyone else. They are standing around, singly or in desultory groups, excited and drinking the Guinness. They like, or dearly wish to like, the music as loud as it is: so loud the thin spines are shaken.

'YOU NEVER LEAVE HIM - YOU LOVE HIM TOO MUCH' thunders the stop-start music. The room is boiling with people, black people, white people, more people; and the wall-lamps turn them all to red, the whole sweating, shuffling crowd. At either end of the bar, in continual danger of being upset, two huge candles stand, their flames startling and glamorous in the semi-darkness. At the bar, on a high stool, sits Marvin, wreathed in blue smoke. He sure is happy tonight. His eyes wander without grudge or urgency among the shapes that swim around him; women in smooth satin blouses, well-dressed strangers sweating at the brow, white guys long-nosed and panting like smiling dogs.

Idly, he notices someone pushing, body by body, through the throng. It is a woman carrying a bulky bundle under one arm. Marvin does not recognize her; he wonders if it is plain-clothes police. Anyone he does not recognize might be police. She is trying to speak to someone but can't make herself heard. People turn back to each other, losing interest in her. But, from the further end of the room, Clyde is making his way towards her. When he reaches her he steers her to the door beside the bar and opens it. They are both close to Marvin; he takes a good look at the woman's face illuminated in the candle-flame. She is younger than he first thought, bossy-looking. He is sure she is a policewoman. Then she and Clyde have gone out the door.

Marvin feels restless, he wants to move. He gets down from his stool and jigs in the head-banging sound-waves. A white girl, his brother's girl, is suddenly beside him. She catches him looking at her and smiles. He gets hot and looks away. He's seen her before; she makes him hot. Now, without warning, she takes his hands in her own and starts to dance with him, pressing close. He moves warily with her, but as he gets hotter he takes courage. He touches her with his fingers. She goes stiff and starts to disengage herself. He holds on harder; she strains against his arms. Suddenly she slackens, wriggles and ducks out from under his arms. As he grabs for her she insinuates herself in the crowd. Clyde comes in and threads his way through to meet her. Marvin is jostled this way and that; he is angry, he feels a fool. Around him teeth flash, smiling, talking, laughing. He feels like smashing them in. He seizes his bottle of whisky from the bar and goes through the door into the passage. The black girl, the policewoman, is coming out of the back room. Josh is holding the door open for her; he sees Marvin. His big voice carries itself through the din. "Hi Marvin! Come here!" Marvin moves forward. Josh cups his mouth and addresses Marvin's ear. "How'd you like to help this young lady sell her papers?"

Marvin shakes his head. "I wanna come watch the game."

"What? You don't want - ? Come on now, a beautiful young lady like this. Look at her!"

"She police," says Marvin.

"What?"

"She police!" he shouts.

Josh laughs. Amazingly the girl laughs too. "She not police, she political," shouts Josh. He likes the sound of this and shouts it again. "She not police, she political!"

The girl looks as if she's remembering something. "You Marvin?" she asks.

"What?" shouts Josh.

She points at Marvin and shouts, "Clyde Harwood's brother?"

Josh nods and laughs. "Yeah, he Clyde's brother. Not much like him, though!"

But she addresses Marvin, as loudly as she can. "Can I talk to you? Somewhere quieter?"

Marvin shrugs his shoulders, rolls up his eyes.

Josh points to the ceiling. "Bathroom upstairs," he says. He lifts his foot and shoves Marvin to the foot of the stairs. "Go on,'" he shouts.

Marvin starts to mount the stairs, into the shadows. The girl is following.

The bathroom is on the next landing, empty, with the light burning. They go in. The music still shakes the floor but other sounds can be heard. Somewhere nearby a child is crying. Marvin closes the toilet lid and sits down. He is mystified, mortified, and still holding his bottle of whisky. Donna, with a sigh of relief, puts her pile of leaflets on the floor and sits on the edge of the bath. She feels in her jacket pocket, brings out cigarettes and offers one to Marvin. He is going to refuse: he would always rather take things than be given them; but changes his mind. Donna lights up both cigarettes and takes a long draw of hers.

"That better."

Marvin smokes in silence. He is on the point of taking a drink from his bottle when an idea comes to him: he offers the bottle to her.

"Have a drink." Surprised, she takes it, tilts it up and drinks. She takes a good drink, Marvin notices, not just a taste. He watches her throat slide daintily under her skin. She hands the bottle back and smiles; she doesn't look bossy any more.

She begins to talk to him. "I heard a lot about you, Marvin, from your brother. My name Donna MacIntyre. I not know if you heard of the group I belong to - New Black Society?"

He doesn't answer.

"- No? Well, I think we might have quite a lot to offer you. I understand you can't get a job -"

Marvin pricks up his ears. "You got a job for me?"

"No, not exactly. New Black Society can't provide jobs - not yet anyway - but we can bring together all local black unemployed people to form a pressure group to force…"

Marvin stops listening. He has no idea why she is talking to him; no idea why he is sitting in this bathroom with her. He likes looking at her, though. Her hair is long and bushy with tortoiseshell ornaments in it like embers of a fire. Her eyes are soulful and intent. They remind him of pictures of the Gospel Choir his mother used to show him. And like the Choir she is dressed in white. But hers is a fluffy, furry white dress that clings to her. Her severe brown jacket can't hide it. Gospel singers never looked like that. She has done herself up for a party even if she does just want to sit in a bathroom and talk.

She is talking and smiling, looking him full in the face. "We all have bad feelings and it right that we should! If only we all put our bad feelings together against whitey, instead of separate, against each other-"

"You get bad feelings?" Marvin interrupts her. He's curious.

She smiles. "Yes man!" She has small teeth; the two front ones are slightly crooked; they gleam for a moment in the dim light. Then her lips close over them.

Marvin is transfixed. "What feelings?" he whispers.

She gives a sudden laugh. "Same as yours, I expect!" She feels tension in the silence between them, and stoops to get a leaflet. "If you like to read this when you get a moment -" but Marvin isn't listening any more. He moves up close to her: there'll be no mistake this time. Donna sees his purpose: this isn't what she wants, it's not what she came for. She bends to pick up the leaflets. "Better get downstairs, give these out." She gathers them laboriously under one arm, with the other hand she opens the door. Marvin tries to stop her but she's halfway out. He struggles with her; the leaflets go down, sliding down the whole flight of stairs. Donna runs down, picking up leaflets as she goes. Marvin follows her, ill with confusion. His feelings are choked in his chest. He watches her crouching and gathering, the severity of her face pronounced again. Anger moves in him. Look at her, engrossed in her pieces of paper! He'll teach her to think so little of him, to turn from him to pieces of paper! "Fuckin' bitch," he snarls. She does not hear but she knows. She reaches the door and bursts into the din of the club-room, but Marvin is still after her. There is no room for her to move: she turns and watches him, her eyes wide and rolling. He feels himself go hard with pleasure as he reaches her; he closes one hand round her neck, then the other. Her breath is squeezed out; she chokes. Her hands and feet fight him as she crashes to the floor, him on top of her. He presses and presses…

Two of the whites get there first; they try to pull Marvin away. Shouting and screaming breaks out; finally the music stops. Josh and Clyde get to Marvin at the same moment. Josh hits Marvin on the back of the neck with the edge of his hand. Marvin stops like a machine switched off and keels over on to his side. They all see Donna lying there, looking like someone who has died in a fight. Josh and Clyde lift her gently and carry her out into the back room. Sylvie is crying as she hovers around Clyde. "Oh, the poor thing; the poor girl," she keeps saying. There is nothing she can do. One of the social workers comes in and says he has had nursing training. "But we should really get her to hospital," he says.

"No!" says Josh and Clyde together.

"She be all right," says Josh. "Listen. She breathing better already."

The social worker listens to her breath and feels her pulse. "It's getting stronger," he admits. "Perhaps it was mainly shock. When she comes round she'll need warm drinks. And we should wrap her in blankets, keep her warm." She is lying, uncovered, on the hard couch.

"We got no blankets," says Josh, "but I got a big rug in the car. You can come get it." He and the social worker go out, leaving Clyde and Sylvie with Donna.

They watch her face. She suddenly opens her eyes and looks straight at Clyde.

"It all right, girl," he whispers.

She closes her eyes again and starts to tremble. Her mouth opens: they can tell she is trying to scream. It comes out finally, weak and croaking. Again and again she croaks, like a chicken held upside-down in the market. Josh comes in with the travelling-rug and packs it around her. The croaking stops; tears run from under her eyelids. All at once she sits up and sobs, crying like a child. Clyde is beside himself to comfort and soothe her enough. He has never pitied anyone so much. The social worker brings a cup of warm milky coffee and Clyde holds it to Donna's lips, time and time again, until she is able to drink some.

* * * * *

Marvin comes to consciousness with the sight of two white strangers crouched beside him. He has a terrible pain in his head; it hurts him to look. But he registers that Clyde isn't there. He doesn't know why his head is aching, nor why he is lying on the floor. He clambers to his feet and staggers.

"Hey now," says one of the strangers. "Take it easy!"

Marvin rocks on his feet and focuses his eyes on a group of figures in front of him. They are looking at him over their shoulders and whispering to each other. One of them catches his eye, turns away and sniggers. Marvin is weakly angry. "Where Clyde?" he asks. A chair is manoeuvred behind him; he sits down in it. Someone gives him a cup of black coffee. He sits sipping, enduring his head and watching the movement around him. The chatter of voices is everywhere; people keep looking at him. Then he hears Josh's voice, "She's all right."

"Great," says one voice; and another, "Thank God for that."

What they talking about, he wonders idly. Josh's voice rises: "Put the music back on, John. Is people still to come." The next minute a blast of music shakes the room, shaking the inside of Marvin's head like strong medicine. He begins to feel better. He gets up and goes towards the bar but he is met by Clyde, Clyde stern and serious, Clyde looking as if he means business.

Clyde takes him by the elbow, pulls him out of the room, down the passage, and out the back door into sudden black darkness. Still his brother holds on as the two of them stumble their way down the unlit junk-yard garden. At the bottom wall they stop. Marvin is shaken and angry. "What the matter? What I do?"

Clyde faces him in the darkness, hating him. "You know what you done to that girl?"

"What girl? I don't know no girls."

"There's a girl in there you tried to strangle. You nearly killed her."

"Me? Not me! You got the wrong man this time, brother. I not touch nobody since I get here. Why you always think it me what make the trouble?"

"Because everybody seen you; because Josh had to hit you to get you off!"

"Josh hit me?"

"Yes! To stop you murdering that girl!"

"Josh hit me." Marvin nods. "That why it hurt so." He puts a hand to the back of his head. "My head. My head hurt."

"Never mind your head. Do you remember what you did?"

"No, I not remember." Marvin taps his foot on a piece of stony rubble. He is losing interest in the conversation. The whites of his eyes flash as he turns to Clyde, suddenly urgent with recollection.

"Hey, I left my bottle of whisky somewhere! Where is it? Yes, man, somebody got it by now!" He starts towards the lights of the house; Clyde makes to follow him, then stops. He rests his weight on the wall and lights a cigarette to calm his nerves.

A doubt comes over him, a familiar doubt. It is doubt of the worth of his efforts. Does he make any difference to Marvin? Is Marvin happy to know that Clyde will stay with him, will take his part whatever he does? Chances are, Marvin neither knows nor cares. What use is Clyde's patience, Clyde's forgiveness? Marvin would be just as happy in prison. He would be neither better nor worse, but the same. A miracle really that such a person can make any sense of life at all. But a hard miracle, because such a person serves the purposes of pain. When Marvin was a child he used to lift their cat onto the red-hot electric hotplate and laugh.

A worn-out anger rises in Clyde: He could thankfully kill Marvin, he hates his brother so much. Ah, but then he pities him again, and is worn out by the trench warfare of his feelings.

He can see Josh silhouetted in the bright doorway: Josh the boss, the one who has saved the girl's life. Marvin will not resent Josh hitting him. To Marvin, Josh is the one who gives money or bangs on the head, it doesn't matter which. Josh comes heavily through the darkness, the sound pounding after him. He has brought a bottle and offers it to Clyde. "Here. You need a drink." Clyde takes a long drink and thanks God for the heat it brings to him. A voice carries from high across the gardens, thin among the mass of the music.

"If you .....turn that thing ... I'm.....-ting the police. .....are trying to sleep.....children here.....fed up with it....." Josh lights a cigarette and stands close so that Clyde will hear him. "Look, I been thinking. That girl, she still pretty nervous. She still scared."

"That don't surprise me."

"Well, now, I think you should take her home. Home to her home, I mean, see if she got somebody there to look after her. If she have nobody, then stay with her. Your white girlfriend as well. Both of you. I talked to her - the girl that got hurt - and she not going to say nothing."

"I never thought she would," said Clyde. "I know her."

"Oh, you know her? That make everything easy. -"

Clyde is suddenly anxious. "Where is she now? Where's Marvin?"

"Relax. Your girlfriend's with her, and that social worker. Errol and Maitland's at the door. Marvin gone with the boys to my place."

"I have to get him home."

"No. See. You take that girl home like I said, you and your white girl, and Marvin can stay at my place tonight. The boys play poker all night anyway."

Clyde relaxes. Josh is good, he gets things done. Clyde feels young and weak beside him.

"I'll get the car," he says.

* * * * *

Donna lived in Forest Gate. Clyde negotiated the streets with care even though they were deserted. He had switched the car-heater on full, and Donna was still wrapped in the thick rug. She sat in the back seat, next to Sylvie. Sylvie wanted to comfort her, and at the same time she was jealous. She took Donna's nearest hand and stroked it in her own.

Clyde asked, "How are you feeling, sweetheart?" And Sylvie only just checked herself from answering. He meant the other girl.

In between noisy breaths Donna replied, "Not bad."

"We'll soon have you home and in bed," Sylvie offered. "We must be nearly there now. Do you recognise this street?"

"Don't ask her," Clyde cut in sharply. "Let her rest. I can find the way all right." For some reason he wanted no-one but himself to tend Donna. Sylvie felt tears gather in her eyes. She withdrew her hand and turned to the dark window. They travelled in silence. Then Donna sat up and pointed. "Here!"

Clyde stopped the car and spoke to Sylvie. "Find her key." He opened the car door and helped Donna out. Sylvie followed miserably, carrying the travelling-rug and the leaflets. They entered a chilly hallway. Donna opened a door and switched on the light of a large, barely furnished room, then stood still, rubbing her neck. Clyde lit the gas fire and drew the curtains. "Sit

69

here for now," he ordered Donna, indicating a shabby leather sofa in the middle of the room. He went out; Sylvie put down the things she was carrying and went after him. In the hallway she stopped him and leaned her head against his shoulder. But he held her away from him. "Make some tea, hey?" he smiled. "And maybe something to eat. I think that's the kitchen." He kissed her on the cheek and went back to Donna. Sylvie wandered into the kitchen. She tried to pull herself together. It was natural he should give his attention to Donna. And perhaps trouble always made him act like this. She beat up some eggs and cooked them, and cut bread and butter for a supper. She laid it all out on a tray and carried it in. Donna's sitting-room was warm and silent; the gas fire burned red, and on the sofa Donna lay sound asleep. On the floor next to her lay Clyde, his head resting upon her. Sylvie put down the tray, not knowing what to do.

Clyde opened his eyes. "Oh, hi. What's that? The supper? All right." He sat up. "We better be quiet, I don't want to wake her." They ate the supper listlessly and then had to decide whether to move Donna. If they lifted her she might waken suddenly, might suffer shock again. "No, we'll leave her here," he said. He studied the sleeping face, the mouth slightly open, the eyelids flickering. How beautiful she was! He had not thought so before tonight.

"Shall we have her bed, then?" Sylvie's voice was unsure, hopeful.

"You go to bed," he said, not looking at her. "If you're tired, you go to bed. I'll come later. I think it's through that door."

So she went alone to the strange bed and lay there, too tired to cry and too miserable to sleep. Some time later she dozed....and awoke with a jump in grey morning light. She left the bed and went into the next room. Clyde was still stretched on the floor beside the sofa, one arm lifted and curved around Donna. One of Donna's hands was resting on Clyde. Both of them were sound asleep and the room was as warm as a warm bed.

* * * * *

After that first night at Donna's, Clyde went there most evenings. It was late when he set out for Forest Gate: he had school work to do earlier, and he always had to check on Marvin's whereabouts. Marvin was always in one of a few familiar places: Josh's, or a club in Graham Street, or one of three pubs, or at home. Clyde did the rounds every evening he went out: he was used to it. He had had the same routine when he used to go to Sylvie's, and before. The few times he had not checked on his brother, Marvin had gone missing, and not returned for days. More than once the police had brought him home. Clyde suspected these occasions were not accidents. Marvin liked Clyde to have to check up on him all the time.

Sometimes when Clyde got to Donna's place she had just come in herself, from a meeting. She had very little to say to him about the meetings. She would frown when he asked, and go to put the kettle on. Once he found her crying silently in the kitchen; she wouldn't tell him why. So he gave up asking her about the group. Instead he spread blankets on the hearth and lay down with her. Her bed was useless to them: it was a narrow single bed in a chilly room. Other girls he had known, like Sylvie, had had double beds. Also they had been on the Pill. Donna had no contraceptive; he had to start buying his own. Her flat was cheerless, too: she had no record-player and only an old television set that was hardly ever switched on. She did not live like other girls: her life seemed silent and austere. She worked as a chief clerk in the office of a container firm on the docks. Only after talking with her gently through many nights did Clyde discover that she gave a large share of her earnings to her mother, who still had children to bring up. They talked a lot about their families and about their childhoods. She nodded and smiled when he told her his mother had been a machinist.

"Yours too?"

"No," she said. "My mother works at the Hackney Hospital. She's a cleaner. But my friends at school, their mothers all did machining. I used to help them pick the bits off the floor after school." She smiled again.

"Where they gone? All your friends?" he asked. "You seem all alone here."

She yawned. "Well, they gone, here and there, you know. Most of them married. All got babies."

"Don't you want babies?" He took her nipple between his fingers.

"Some time," she smiled at him, relaxed.

"But not yet?"

Her face lost its openness and took on the severity he remembered from the old times. "Is more important things to do," she said, in the same kind of voice. "We should give our energy, while we're young, to getting the new society going. Anyway is plenty children around already, needing care."

"Well all right," he said. "If that's how you feel, bring one home. Adopt one."

"Don't be crazy . I can't. I on my own. A child couldn't live here. That not what I mean."

"What do you mean, then?"

"I mean we can provide for children in other ways. We can work for them."

He was silent. She seemed not to make any connections. He was forced to say, "But you do work for them already. You told me you help to support your mother's children."

"That not the same. That my family. That natural."

"So you mean it's not worth anything unless it's not natural?"

"In a way, yes." She sat up. "We got to make an effort more than that."

He considered. "Well, I teach other people's children. That's not natural. Why don't you do that?"

"But you get paid for it. That just your job. Anyway you teach white kids."

"I teach white and black. What wrong with that?"

"I tell you what wrong with it!" Her voice rose, she knew where she was now. "*Our* efforts should be for *our* society! Whitey has had the best of everything! It our people's turn now! Now we have plenty of black teachers they should teach black kids!"

"But how can they? We not living in an all-black country. All the schools are mixed."

"If we start an all-black school will you teach in it?"

"Yes, if you want." But he wasn't so sure. "You know, a lot of white kids need helping, too. I feel just as bad about them."

"Not me!" But she wasn't so sure, either. She had known some wretched white children when she was little herself. She lay back on the blankets, her energy spent. "I don't know. The group has some good ideas. You confuse me."

"I'm sorry," said Clyde and got up.

"Oh no!" she cried. "Don't take it like that! I not mean it your fault! I just mean.....I don't know.....I seem to see too many things at once."

He laughed and went back to her. "So do I. You have the same effect on me! I just thinking now. If we

74

lived in an all-black society we wouldn't have to pick and choose among the kids. We could feel the same way about them all."

"So?" She was thoughtful, trying to pick up his idea.

"You ever been back to Jamaica?" he asked. "Shall we go there someday, you and me?"

"Jamaica! Why?"

"Well, it where we come from, our families, in the first place. And it a black country."

"It's not, it's mixed, same as here."

"But got a black government."

"Yes, I know. But I don't know how much difference....." she couldn't put it into words.

"Come on!" said Clyde. "Your group should know about these things. There's good signs in Jamaica right now."

"You talking about the entente with Cuba? But that all old- style politics!" She had got it out, finally. "That not what we want! We want a new beginning, new ideas - what about Africa?"

"All right, Donna" Clyde got up definitely this time and put his clothes on. "You do what you like. I'm going now."

"Why?" She was afraid she had driven him away.

"Why do you think?" He turned his mouth down at the corners.

"Your brother?"

"Yes. He gone to a card-game in Clapton. I said I'd pick him up."

She was silent, contemplating his responsibility. He would never be free of it.

"How is he?" she asked quietly. She got up and put on her dressing-gown, started to fold up the blankets.

"He all right," said Clyde at the door, ready to go.

"He ever say anything about - ?"

"No, he don't say nothing about it. When I ask him he say he don't remember. Maybe he don't."

"Maybe not," she whispered, her head drooped. She knew he was going now. But unexpectedly he closed her in his arms.

"Donna. Girl. Be for me and you," he said into her hair.

She leaned against him and shed tears. "I am, I am!"

And she was. The harder she argued with him the more she felt he was right.

She was constrained now at the meetings of New Black Society, and it was not just the old constraint of the others not liking her. It was the constraint of being private in a public place. She had told them nothing about Clyde, or the club, or Marvin's attack upon her. She told them she had not gone to any clubs that night. As the weeks went by she contributed less and less at discussions, and caught herself daydreaming when papers were being read. From being an argumentative member of the group she dropped to being a silent hanger-on. And after Christmas, which she spent at her mother's, she did not go to any more meetings.

* * * * *

Clyde drove home from school one day in January to find a man waiting at the door. He knew the man: it was a social worker whose job was to visit families 'at risk'. Clyde and Marvin were 'at risk'. Marvin was 'at risk' whenever he stopped being on probation. He had never yet been to jail. Keeping him out was Clyde's big achievement.

The social worker turned at the slam of the car door. He was a thin white guy with broken veins in his cheeks and strings of straight hair blowing loose from his bald head. Sometimes a different social worker came: a boy in a denim suit who said 'Yeah man.' Marvin treated them with the same indifference.

"Is Marvin in?" asked the social worker.

"Should be," said Clyde, pushing the door. It was locked. Clyde unlocked it. "That's strange. He didn't say he was going out."

The social worker, whose name was Pritchard, followed him into the living-room and sat down in a ragged armchair.

"How is he getting on?"

"Marvin? No different from last time." Clyde did not even consider telling the guy about Marvin's attack on Donna. The guy offered no remedy, none of them did, so why should they see the sores? Clyde had no impulse to confide in people, certainly not in social workers, probation officers and such. Their professional interest in misery repelled him. And they had no remedy.

"Don't you think," began Pritchard, "that we should try again to get him employed, now the new year has started?"

Clyde was unresponsive. "Try if you like. Only if anything goes wrong, make sure the bosses get on to you this time, not me."

"Well, yes, I'm willing to take responsibility. Though Marvin never *does* get in touch with me, even when things go wrong."

"No, he doesn't, it's always me. Still -" Clyde feigned interest. "What job do you think you can get him?"

"Oh I haven't anything definite in mind. Just on principle, I think he ought to work. For his self-respect."

"For Marvin's self-respect, yeah." Clyde's voice was weary.

All at once the door opened and Marvin came in. He looked at his brother and Pritchard with no surprise. He took off his coat and faced Clyde. "I not be here much longer. I moving out."

Clyde was unpacking his books onto the table. He stopped. "What did you say?"

"I said I moving out." He stood in front of the mirror and studied his face.

"Moving out? What you mean? What you talking about?"

Marvin did not answer. He studied his face in the mirror, opening his mouth and examining his teeth.

"Marvin! I talking to you! What you mean, you moving out? Where you going? What idea is this?"

"I going to Josh's."

"Josh's? What, to live?"

"Yeah."

Clyde took a deep breath to control the feelings that rushed at him from every direction, colliding with each other.

"Why? When did you see him?"

"I see him all the time, you know that. Just been there now."

"You can't mean it. You can't just leave. You can't look after yourself."

Marvin gave his solicitous brother a straight look. "I can look after my fuckin' self the way I want to. And Josh got work for me to do. He fix it all up. He get me a girl, he pay me good." His enthusiasm had made him confide more than usual. Regretting it, he shut up his face and stood picking his fingernails. Pritchard, impotent, looked from one to the other of them, his mouth slightly open, soundless.

"What girl? What pay? What work?"

But Marvin had done talking. Clyde stood in front of him, trying to force his attention.

"Now Marvin, you listen to me! Working for Josh ain't any good for you! I don't say nothing against him, only that he ain't any good for you!" But he was not whole-hearted. He knew what Josh could do, he had seen it. He went on talking, without conviction. "You stay home. We'll find you a job if you want to work."

"Leave me be!" Marvin knocked his brother's hands away. His voice rose.

"I don't do what you say no more! I sick of you! I sick of living here! Josh know me, he know what I want!"

Pritchard's flat nasal tones broke in. "Who is Josh, Marvin?"

Marvin ignored him. He faced Clyde. "You no good to me, brother! You make me worse 'n what I am!"

"He may have something there!" Pritchard again.

Clyde turned away; Marvin had hit him on the raw.

"Marvin may be right!" Pritchard enlarged to the unlistening, disregarding air. "Perhaps it is time he made a break. He might be happier with someone else. And if his friend can employ him to…What work would you be doing, Marvin?"

Marvin had not finished with his brother yet. He caught Clyde's eye and held it steadily. "You don't want me here. Don't kid me, I know. Well, I don't wanna be here either. You're a drag on me, too."

Clyde felt stunned with admiration. How intelligent his brother could be! "Okay then, Marvin," he replied. "If that's how you feel. Go then. Let's hope Josh is better for you than I've been."

"He will be," said Marvin. He moved about the room, picking up objects and examining them, gathering a few together, whistling under his breath. Carrying the things he had chosen he went upstairs.

Pritchard's voice ground on. "I wonder if it isn't rather sudden? It might be better to talk it over and find out his exact plans. I'm all in favour of him being independent, of course, but we ought to make sure it will be a change for the better…"

The room was empty: Clyde had followed his brother upstairs.

* * * * *

Marvin did move out. He went to live in one of the flats in Josh's Camleigh Road house, the house that had the club in the basement. For days after he had left, Clyde felt strange in the empty house, drifting from room to room, effortless and weightless. He had not expected such sudden relief. It was nothing like his fantasies of life without Marvin. Those fantasies had taken no account of the strangeness of it. Not for years had he had a holiday away from his brother, not since their mother had died. He hardly knew what to do with himself now, unburdened.

He did not feel the benefit of his freedom until the first time he stayed with Donna a whole night. He began to feel it then, and to be alert in anticipation of all the space and time he could enjoy. He moved into it, hesitantly at first, like someone learning to swim, then confidently. He enlarged the scope of his life.

Donna stayed the whole night with him once, at his house, and then again, and then for the weekend. During this time he saw nothing of Marvin or Josh, nor did he want to. He knew he would have to go and see them some time, but he pushed the thought aside, it was loathsome to him. He was light-headed and determined to keep his freedom.

He wanted Donna to move in with him, but she was afraid of meeting Marvin again. She was afraid every time she came to the house and jumped if a car-door slammed outside. Clyde did not like her fear: it seemed she did not trust him to protect her, and he was feeling omnipotent. He insisted, and in the end she came. Clyde was suddenly a winner. He grew drunk on it. His school work palled on him: he wanted nothing but leisure. He bought a double bed and they spent whole weekends in it, getting up in the evening to go out for a meal, coming straight home and into the bed again.

Donna relaxed. She lived in a dream, dawdling over her typing at the warehouse, throbbing suddenly as she saw him out of the window, waiting for her in the car.

She went to see her mother one evening, and told her she was living with a man. Her mother, resting her feet and heavy legs on a stool, looked at her suspiciously. "You gettin' a baby?"

"No."

"Ah. Will be soon, though, if you livin' with a man. You not lose your job, did you?"

"No, I still got the job. Matter of fact I might be able to give you a bit more money now I don't have my rent to pay. I see how it goes and I give you some more if I can."

"You get a baby, you have to stop working. I can't start lookin' after another."

"I won't have a baby; don't you worry about that."

"How you know you won't?" She lowered her voice. "Does he use them things?"

Donna nodded, looking at the floor.

Her mother seemed satisfied with this.

"What sort of man is him?"

"A teacher."

"A teacher! Well, that good. He got much money?"

"No, but he got enough. It his own house."

"Just him there? He got no family?"

Donna replied slowly. "He got a brother. But he moved out."

"He a teacher as well? The brother?"

"No." She took a deep breath. "He work in a club.

"In a club? A teacher brother? It sound queer to me. Did you meet him? Hm? Donna, I ask you a question! Did you meet him brother?"

"Yes, once. -" She halted, then hurried. "But only for a little while. Do you want a cup of coffee? I think I make some." She moved out to the kitchen.

"Tea for me," called her mother.

When Donna brought the drinks in her mother said, "Well, I surprised by you, Donna. I thought you was different from other girls, with your politics an' all. Now you tell me you livin' with a man just like everybody else."

Donna stirred her coffee. Her mother had touched her most sensitive spot.

"Well, you make sure he treat you right!" her mother admonished, as they sipped and warmed themselves at the fire. "Don't get no baby and don't lose your job!"

Donna unpacked the treats she had brought for the children and put them on the table. Then she kissed her mother. "I'll come again soon," she promised. She left and walked to the corner of the street where Clyde was waiting for her in the car.

* * * * *

Josh had given Marvin a flat on the top floor of the Camleigh Road house. The flat below was occupied by a white family with two little children. The woman of this family lived in fear of fire. Before she went to bed every night she crept up and down the staircases, sniffing for smoke. She awoke, panicking, in the night, thinking she smelled it. She woke her husband too, which irritated him. He could never smell any burning.

Fire engines shrieked through those streets every day. One winter night a house went up in flames, burning to death a ten- month-old baby, while his mother crawled among blinding, blistering furniture, searching for him, screaming her way to madness. And a girl, the baby's sister, escaped into the street with sheets of burned skin hanging off her arms.

The woman in the flat below Marvin had seen it all from the window, and speechless fear took its first handhold on her brain. She became afraid for her own two children. At weekends she took them to stay with her sister in Bethnal Green. Her husband came with them sometimes, but he grudged the fares. They had been in Camleigh Road for over four years and still it was not their turn for a council house. She had grown accustomed to the din from the club, the broken nights. Her children were inured to it and could remember nothing else. She was used to trembling in the street when she had to pass the numerous, slinking, savage stray dogs. But fire was for her the final evil: the one she would not be able to face, the one that would win.

And it came. It sprang from Marvin's heater by way of a magazine page that drifted over the top vents. It fell sideways with the burning, curling page on to a heap of loose papers. There was no-one in the room to stop it: it ran amok, caught clothes, travelling along the bed-covers. It climbed a table-leg, and taking hold, stood up tall flames which reached to the patchy ceiling and its bare laths. It took possession of the room and approached the half-open door. A hand of flame closed on the door's lowest corner; the whole mass followed. Inside an hour it went berserk through the top floor and was beyond stopping. Then it burst through the roof and made its presence known.

The woman in the flat below - but thank God, it was Saturday night, they were all at Bethnal Green. Marvin was out too, and so was the girl who lived in the next room. Even the Irishman on the ground floor was out. The club was closed: Josh was operating one of his other clubs that night.

So it was that the white woman and her family, returning from Bethnal Green on Sunday evening, rounded the corner into Camleigh Road and found the top of the house gone. They went inside, and the stairs were black with soot. The walls of the upstairs landing were wet and smelled of fire. Their flat was soaked, the furniture ruined. The woman cried with relief, her fear dead. The evil had come out of hiding, had ravaged the house and not caught them. The man was secretly offended that his judgment had been wrong. He went around the house, tapping walls, belittling the fire. They set out for the police-station, not knowing what else to do, the woman strangely light-hearted as she shut the front door behind her. She had good reason. They were given a council house before the end of the month.

* * * * *

Josh was sourly angry about the fire. He did not laugh when the news came to him. He liked to let things happen, to see how they turned out, but not when they happened to him, not when they were things like this. His club in Palatine Street was in full swing that Saturday night, he himself the centre of the thickest crowd, Sylvie beside him, when Maitland pushed his way through to tell of the fire in Camleigh Road. The smile was wiped off Josh's face; he left his revels and drove straight away to the burning house. When he saw only the top floor blazing he knew who had done it. The street was full of people watching the flames and fire- hoses. Josh identified himself to the police and answered questions about the tenants. "Have you any idea how it could have started?" they asked him.

"Yeah," he replied. "I know how it started."

He drove back to Palatine Street and sought out Marvin from a far corner of the club. He dragged him upstairs by the collar of his shirt, struggling and complaining, and into a room used for card-games. He threw Marvin into a chair and stood in front of him, his burly body tense with anger. His breath came in short gasps, he jabbed the air with a short, strong forefinger, pointing. His voice was quiet, leashed back.

"You in real trouble, boy!" He could not get his words together, his anger choked him." *You* done that fire! You burn my house!"

Open-mouthed, Marvin gawked at him, then began to shake his head. "No! Not me, boss! I not do it!"

"Shut your mouth!" Josh hit him across the face, raised his hand to hit again, but stopped and let it fall.

He might kill the kid if he started. He shouted instead, a deep roar that even Errol heard, at the foot of the stairs, in spite of the music.

"That fuckin' heater! How many times I tell you about it? That fuckin' thing set the fuckin' house on fire!"

Still Marvin gaped, uncomprehending and terrified.

"That heater in your room!" roared Josh, and people just coming into the club stopped talking and looked up the stairs. ("It all right," said Errol. "He teachin' somebody a lesson.")

Marvin's face showed the beginning of enlightenment.

"*My* heater?"

"Yes, your heater! It start a fire at the house! The top of the house all burned away! Fire engines is there now, police too!"

Marvin understood. "A fire? Is my things all right?"

Josh halted, his flow of anger confused. "Your things? What you talking about, man? You crazy! Everything burned up, everything gone!"

Marvin nodded. "I knowed it. I should have left my things at home. They safe there."

Josh was repelled; it was like trying to talk to a child. He turned his back. "You got to get out," he said, not shouting any more. "You got to leave my house. I don't want you around no more. Go back to your brother, I don't want to see you no more." He went through the door and down the stairs. But Marvin ran after him, followed him downstairs, ran in front of him, flung himself around his legs. He begged for another chance, he begged Josh not to throw him out.

"I do anything for you, boss! I mend the house! I get it all clean again!"

There was a moment's lull in the music. People crowded through the doorway and into the hall, trying to see what was happening on the stairs. "Go back '" Josh told them. "It nothing here. Tell John to start the music again." To Marvin he said, "Leave me be. Get up. You get me mad enough for one night."

"Boss, I not want to go!" bawled Marvin, drowning in the sudden overwhelming flood from the sound system. Josh looked down on him, seeing his mouth form words. "I mend the house! Let me stay!"

He was irritated beyond bearing. He nodded once, brusquely, to shut the kid up, to get rid of him. He would talk to him properly tomorrow. He nodded again. "Yes, yes."

Marvin, watching his face, understood. He smiled widely, then got up and carefully dusted his jacket and trousers free of the dirt they had picked up while he was kneeling. Without a backward glance he returned to the club-room.

The talk the following day was the same: he persuaded Josh to let him stay. Josh told himself that since the cost of repairing the house would be high, he might as well let Marvin act as a labourer. Perhaps it would only need one skilled man, if Marvin did the labouring. He could sleep on the couch in the back room of the club until the work was finished. So Marvin was moved down into the basement. He could no longer watch the comings and goings in the street, of course. He had better do good work on the house, to earn his keep, Josh decided. And there was, after all, the insurance.

Marvin didn't do good work. Lester, the jack-of-all-trades hired to do the repairs, complained to Josh about him. He wouldn't listen when he was shown how to do things, he spoiled every job he was given, he wasted materials. There were times when Josh called at the club unexpectedly and found Marvin sitting at the bar, drinking whisky, dropping ash on the floor. Josh lost his temper, but Marvin dodged off the stool and ran out. Later he would be sorry, and beg Josh to come and see the work he had done. Josh resolved to send him back to Clyde; he was not amused any more.

* * * * *

Donna's former comrades from New Black Society came to the house one night. They wanted to talk to her. She had known they would come sooner or later.

"You don't come to group meetings any more," Clark, the leader, began.

"No," said Donna, bringing them into the sitting room.

"We went round to your address four or five times before we found out that you had moved," another of them put in. This was Umtale, a Kenyan student. "Finally we rang up your workplace. They told us your new address."

"Sit down," she said. "We won't be disturbed for a while." Clyde was upstairs having a bath. But they remained standing.

"We would like an explanation," said Clark.

"I'm sorry," she said, and immediately wished she had not. She was determined not to be put on the defensive. "All I have to say is that something has happened. My attitude has changed towards New Black Society."

"What has happened?" asked Umtale.

"That is private to me."

"I suppose you mean you have fallen in love," sneered Clark, looking at the masculine clothes hanging over a chair. "Who is it? A white man?"

Donna was stung. "No it isn't! But what if I have fallen in love? I don't have to excuse myself to you!"

They were startled. The girl who was with them looked at Donna open-mouthed, then swallowed and looked away.

Donna appealed to them. "Look, you've got to take what I say! If I've fallen in love, or whatever I've done, it's my life! You've got to take it, people have real lives!"

"We know people have real lives." It was Umtale, he spoke gently. "But people do not always understand their experience. We would like to help you to understand your experience, whatever it is. That's what the group is for, to enlighten the people. You should not need me to tell you this. When people understand their experience they will join our numbers."

"Numbers!" burst out Donna. "You so concerned with numbers, aren't you?"

"No," cut in Clark. "Recruiting membership is a means to an end, not the end itself."

"So you say!" retorted Donna. "But tell me this. Why you come to see me? Is it because you wonder why I left? Do you wonder why the group won't do for me any more? Or are you angry at losing a member?" She did not wait for an answer. "Yes, that why you here! That why you want me to say sorry! You think I ought to feel guilty about leaving - "

"Why did you join in the first place?" snapped Clark, narrow- eyed.

Donna got her breath back. "Because I wanted to do something about being black," she answered at length. "The group was the best thing I could think of then."

"Aren't you black any more?" Clark's eyes flashed. "Don't the whites put you down any more? Don't you want to be with your own people, against the enemy?"

"Yes, I do! I do want to and I am! It's just-" the sheaf of leaflets the girl was carrying caught her eye, "all these leaflets! All these meetings! They don't seem to do anything!"

"You were keen enough on leaflets not long ago," said Clark, with sarcasm. "You begged to write them yourself, if I remember."

She was glad that Umtale broke in. He was indignant.

"What do you mean - all these leaflets? How else are we to reach people? We cannot buy television time."

Donna turned to him. "It would be no different if you could! It would be just another TV programme! Same as now you're like - the Jehovah Witnesses or something, tryin' to get members!"

"And how do *you* propose we make contact with people?" Clark again."Or don't you think it's necessary? Do you think we should all stay in our separate miseries till God comes down and sorts it out?"

"No, I don't. What I'm sayin' is we don't have to *make* contact, we *got* contact! Already! All the time! We not livin' on a cloud in the sky! We got people round us all the time, we ought to be a new black society with *them*. Instead of havin' meetings every week, all talk -"

"I don't think you're making a lot of sense '" Clark interrupted, cold and casual. "What exactly do you mean by 'being a new black society with them'? What is entailed in being a new black society is precisely what we talk about at meetings. But maybe you know how to do it already? Maybe you know more than the rest of us. Have you any ideas about jobs for teenagers, for instance?"

"No, but neither have you! Except for more meetings and - "

"Okay! All right!" Clark held up a dismissive hand. "I don't think there can be any further useful dialogue between us." He moved towards the door. The girl member, who had remained wordless all this time, moved with him. But Umtale was not satisfied.

"Suppose we did away with the organization," he said to Donna, "and suppose people nevertheless made political contact with each other, as I understand you to suggest, would that not still leave them powerless in a time of crisis? Who would be the leaders? How could any striking force operate?"

"The striking force would be everybody. An uprising," Donna answered, but she knew she was answering wildly. She was on shaky ground, but pressed on. "I don't know about leaders. I expect they'd be the same people they always are."

"Who?"

"Them that want it most."

"Come away, Umtale, it's no use." Clark held the door open. The girl made as if to place a leaflet on the table, but he stopped her. "It's no use," he repeated. He held the door open for the girl and Umtale to go out, then turned his back and left without another word.

Donna stood staring at the closed door. She was trembling with stimulation, on the verge of tears. In the suddenly quiet house she heard Clyde's bare feet padding down the stairs. He came into the room with a towel wrapped around his waist. His face was warm and smiling.

"Who was that? I heard you shouting." He looked at her more closely. "Hey, baby, what is it? What happened?"

She strove to keep her voice steady. "Nothing. It was the group. I been expecting them. We had an argument."

"Oh, the group. Ha! Who won?"

"I don't know. I think I did. I suppose they think they did. Clyde, get me a fag, will you? I need it."

He searched the room for a packet and found one with three in, flattened and dry. He lit up for both of them. They sat side by side on the battered settee, smoking. Finally Donna relaxed and leaned her face against his bare, smooth shoulder.

They now had nothing but each other and their daily work. Clyde's friends from school and from the neighbourhood had stopped coming around, they saw he was bored with them; he yawned over the cards and didn't take in what they said. He was even beginning to lose interest in his teaching. His time with Donna was all he cared about, yet he knew they shouldn't live like this, wrapped up in each other, drifting away from everything else. He began to take the idea of Africa seriously. They talked about going, in a casual, guarded way; they got books out of the library. Finally, one night they pledged they would go. They would give up their jobs and go. Dizzy with commitment, their passion for each other only increased the more, as if it could embrace a whole continent.

* * * * *

Then they heard about the fire. They knew instantly who had started it. They each knew, separately and instantly, but they did not talk about it together. It broke their union, they could not talk about it together. And they each knew separately what would result from the fire: Marvin would come back. It was impossible to talk about such a thing. Equally, it became impossible to talk about going to Africa. They said nothing, became hollow-eyed. First Donna, and then Clyde, caught flu. On a day when Clyde was at the launderette and Donna in bed ill, Josh found Clyde and told him, there and then, that he was sending Marvin back. "You damn' lucky I not take you to court," he said. And on another day a week or two later, when Clyde was in bed and Donna recovering, Marvin came back, whistling, one hand in his pocket, the other swinging his suitcase.

Donna was standing in the kitchen holding two mugs of coffee when she heard the footsteps and the whistling. She had made coffee for Clyde to swallow his tablets with. Now she put the mugs down and looked at Marvin in fear.

Marvin recognised her and abruptly shut his mouth. Why was *she* here? She had no right to be standing in the kitchen, making him feel upset. He scowled and turned his face aside. "Where's Clyde?"

Donna opened her mouth, but her voice would not come.

He glanced at her with bright, irritable eyes. "I said, 'Where's Clyde?'"

"In...in the bedroom. He's in bed. He's ill."

He grunted and went out of the kitchen, leaving his suitcase on the floor. Donna picked up the cups of coffee and put them down again, her hands shaking and slopping the coffee. But Clyde must have his medicine, Marvin or not. She put the bottle of tablets in her jeans pocket and carried the cups resolutely up the stairs. Clyde was propped up on one elbow, coughing into a handkerchief. Marvin was standing at the foot of the bed, fingering the covers.

"You changed it all round," he accused. "Where your other bed?"

Clyde, heaving and spitting, was unable to answer him. Marvin waited until Clyde drew breath and repeated, "Clyde! Where your other bed?"

"What you sayin', man?" gasped his brother.

"I sayin', 'Where your other bed?'"

"What other bed, what you sayin'?" He closed his mouth and, lifting his hand, slowly rubbed his neck.

"Your other bed. What you used to have in here. It gone, where is it?"

"I moved it into your room," whispered Clyde, but the cough came back. When he had finished he lay back in bed and took the tablets that Donna silently held out.

"Into my room?" continued Marvin. "Does that mean that I can have it?"

They both looked at him. "Have what?" asked Donna.

"That bed," said Marvin. "Now it in my room, can I have it? It better than mine. Mine had some springs broken."

Donna felt the blood rush to her face, dissolving her fear. "How can you talk to Clyde about such things? Can't you see he's ill?"

"I know he ill," snapped Marvin. "I know him better than you; he my brother."

"Well then, can't you behave like a brother?"

"What it got to do with you?" His voice, rough and loud, filled up the cramped room. "What you doing here anyway? You not live here!"

"Yes I do!" Her voice was loud too. "I live here now! And I won't let you talk like that to Clyde when he's ill!"

"Talk like what? It you that shouting, woman, not me! Clyde!" he turned his head, ignoring her, "Clyde, can I have that other bed of yours that you move into my room?"

Clyde turned his head this way and that on the pillow. "You're all roaring," he cried. "Yes, have the bed. And get out now, I want to sleep. You too, Donna. Leave me be." His eyes closed, frowning.

But Marvin turned back when he reached the door. "Oh Clyde, Josh want to know if you can pay something for the repairs for that fire. He say it my fault. It weren't my fault but he say it was and he want you to pay something for the repairs. I tell him it weren't my fault-"

"Come out and leave him alone!" whispered Donna furiously.

"Clyde!" called Marvin, his hand on the door.

But all that came from the bed was a groan and a muffled cough that made the blankets shake. Breathing hard with annoyance Marvin went out, slamming the door, and downstairs to get his suitcase.

In the kitchen Donna was washing up. Marvin stared at her, taking in the novelty and insult of her presence. Why had no-one told him she would be here? Josh had never told him. Clyde had not told him, the times he came round. They were all his enemies. He watched her, her arms moving busily, her body not quite still as she worked in the sink. It was hard to believe she was the same one. Last time he had looked at that body she had been lying down.

She glanced up to see him staring at her. She bent her head to her task and tried to ignore him. He turned abruptly and picked up his suitcase. When he came downstairs again his mood had changed.

"That room crowded with two beds in it," he complained. "He have to take the other one out." He moved a step nearer. "Are you going cook something?"

Donna was disconcerted; she did not know what tone to use with him.

"I don't know. Clyde can't keep anything down and I've not much appetite yet. I've had flu as well."

"Well I hungry," said Marvin. "Last thing I had to eat was last night."

"Do you want to cook yourself something?" asked Donna uncertainly. She remembered she had not taken her own tablet yet.

"What you got in?" demanded Marvin, throwing open all the cupboards. "Nothin' but fuckin' eggs! He know I not like eggs!"

"He didn't know you was coming back today!" Again Donna was angered out of her fear of him. "We been ill, we not been buying food!"

"He know I not like fuckin' eggs!" muttered Marvin, kicking the door shut.

"Go out and get something, then," said Donna. "Get something from the shops." She was feeling worse: she must take her tablet and lie down. She gave him a pound and some silver out of her purse. "Here. Get yourself something and cook it."

"What shall I get?"

"How do I know? What you want! Get what you want!"

"Shall I get pork chops?"

"Yes, if you like them!"

"Yeah. I like pork chops. Clyde cook them real nice for me."

"But he can't cook today! He's ill!"

"Yeah, that right." Marvin considered. "He could maybe just cook the chops and then go back to bed."

"I'll cook them for you," said Donna, weary. "Just go get them."

When he had gone she took her tablet and lay down beside Clyde. She breathed deeply to try and calm herself, but the exhaling juddered and turned to tears. She tried to cry silently, but Clyde turned and put his arm around her. "Never mind, girl" he gasped. "We think of something."

But she had had enough. "It's no good. Thinking won't do any good. There's no hope for us." The words came in loud jagged sobs. "We won't ever get to Chad, or Dahomey, or anywhere. We'll never get away. He's the black society we're going to give our lives to!" She just cried, openly, defeated. And Clyde said nothing. There was nothing; she was right. And not just for them. In the end, in the last analysis, there was no pattern or purpose, effort was not rewarded or even noticed. It would probably have been the same if they had gone to Africa. That too would have proved to be beyond them, intractable. And yet Clyde realized he meant to stay alive. Something was being a source of comfort, of hope; something must be, or else he would be working out how to kill himself. It was her, it was being with her.

"Stay with me, Donna," he whispered.

"I've no choice," she cried. "I've given up everything else."

After a moment he asked "But don't you love me any more?"

She kissed his face to reassure him, and herself. "Yes, I still love you. I just wish -"

"I know. So do I. Go if you want to."

The front door banged.

"Clyde!" shouted Marvin.

Donna sighed and wiped her face. "I'm corning," she called. "Clyde can't." They heard Marvin move into the kitchen. Slowly she tidied herself and went downstairs. In the kitchen Marvin was standing in front of the stove, from which rose blue smoke.

"What are you doing?" she asked wearily. "Move out the way." He half-turned his head and relinquished the frying-pan handle. Through the smoke, at the bottom of the pan, two huge pale chops could be seen. Gas-flames grew up around the outside of the pan like fiery grass. She turned down the gas.

"Nobody came to cook them," said Marvin, "so I cooked them myself."

"Marvin," she said, "you must learn to wait. It wasn't for long." Perhaps the answer was to treat him like a child. She turned the chops over and seasoned them.

He was watching her over her shoulder, breathing down her neck. "Hey," he said softly, "what was you doin' upstairs? You an' him?" He sniggered. She felt her skin crawl, and held on tight to the pan -handle. Treat him like a child.

"That none of your business," she said lightly.

"Ha. You was doin' it up, wasn't you? You was doin' it up with him." He touched her back with his hand.

"That's enough!" Donna twisted away from him. "Get a plate for your food."

But he stayed right where he was, close to her. He said "I know you."

"What do you mean?"

"You was at Josh's that night. We was in a bathroom together."

"Now listen, Marvin!" she turned on him. "If you and me are going to live here we'll have to get a few things straight! You don't talk about that time, you don't even think about it! You try to show me you're sorry!" Her hand crept up to her neck.

Watching it, his face altered; he snarled. "It not me, I never done that to you!" He hated her for bringing such things up.

There was a silence filled by the spluttering of the chops. Donna put them on a plate. Marvin sat gracelessly to the table. His stomach was sour: she had spoiled his appetite. He pushed the meat around his plate, grimacing as he chewed. Donna sat and talked to him. She asked him about Josh's house, about jobs he'd had. It choked Marvin. She didn't fool him, trying to act like his mother. His mother hadn't looked like that. He looked at her from under hooded eyes as she talked. He returned monosyllables and watched her.

* * * * *

In the days that followed Donna was always careful. She knew she must be; she could not afford to relax in her own home. Fear and loathing of Marvin alternated with pity, for him, for Clyde, for herself; and all feelings began to be coloured with despair,with the raw ochre of knowing that the world was incomprehensible. If she and Clyde made love, it was desperately, in moments when Marvin was not at home and they were. She could not bear it much longer, but did not know what else to do. If not this, what could she bear? Was she, after all, like so many she had criticised in the past, no good at anything except theories? An excellent pamphleteer? But, in the end, it began not to matter. Misery was misery: explanations and resolutions made no difference. And at this low point, when she had become careless through weariness, and when Marvin might indeed have killed her - and forgotten about it the next day - it was gradually borne in on her that he was spending less time at home. Clyde did not notice it at first, but when she mentioned it to him, wonderingly, he paid more attention to his brother's comings and goings.

"Don't ask him outright," Donna warned. "Don't let him know we've noticed. There's another thing," she went on. "His room smells of ganja. He don't eat pork chops any more. I think he joined the Rastas."

Neither of them saw, separately or together, where it might end - Marvin joining the Rastas, if indeed he had. They were just glad of the present relief. Clyde had grown used, over the years, to expecting nothing more. The whole time Donna had stayed with him felt like a luxury; he knew that in the last analysis he was as entitled to such a thing as anyone else, but he knew from experience that he was not. As for going to Africa!

So, precariously glad of the unexpected free evening they had just had, they stood together at the window one night, relaxed, the curtains a little drawn back, watching the rain in the street lights, and wondering where Marvin was. They were about to turn away when they saw some figures moving up from the end of the street, one slightly ahead of the others. They watched as the little band approached, slowly. In front was the ragged man with the flute, playing. Three young men behind him, one of them Marvin, were doing a stately dance, formal and ceremonial, in the rain. Their hair was in fantastic locks, like the manes of black lions; except Marvin's, which had not had time to grow yet. But he danced as well as the others. As they danced they passed a smoke from one to the other. They kept pausing to relight it. No-one seemed impatient.

Clyde and Donna, absorbed in the strangeness of the spectacle, felt a sudden but familiar sinking of the heart as the dancers reached their door. Now the spell would be broken. Marvin, once home, would be as he always was. Minutes passed. The flute-player shook his flute and lifted it again to his mouth. The group moved on. It had moved on; the streetlight catching the bright raindrops on their lion-manes. A slight tang of ganja came through the closed window as Clyde and Donna watched the backs of the dancers, including Marvin. They had gone away down the street and Marvin had gone with them, without stopping, without even looking at his own front door. Simultaneously Clyde and Donna looked away from the window and at each other, outlined in a pale, unwatched-for dawn of hope.